Water Lily

Also by Susanna Jones

The Earthquake Bird

Water Lily

Susanna Jones

Published by Warner Books

An AOL Time Warner Company

Copyright © 2003 by Susanna Jones
All rights reserved.

This Mysterious Press edition is published by arrangement with Picador, an imprint of Pan Macmillan Ltd, 20 New Wharf Road, London N1 9RR, UK.

 Mysterious Press books are published by Warner Books, Inc.,
1271 Avenue of the Americas, New York, NY 10020.

Visit our Web site at www.twbookmark.com.

 An AOL Time Warner Company

The Mysterious Press name and logo are registered trademarks of Warner Books, Inc.

Printed in the United States of America

First Mysterious Press Printing: March 2003
10 9 8 7 6 5 4 3 2 1

Library of Congress Cataloging-in-Publication Data

Jones, Susanna.
    Water lily / Susanna Jones.
        p. cm.
    ISBN 0-89296-776-5
    1. Lake District (England)—Fiction. 2. Asians—England—Fiction. 3. Women immigrants—Fiction. 4. Married people—Fiction. 5. Murderers—Fiction. I. Title.

PR6110.O64 W3 2003
823'.92—dc21   2002032161

BOOK I

One

Runa arrived at her sister's house in the dark. The wooden building, not much more than a shed with a few scrubby bushes in front, was lit dimly by a couple of vending machines at the end of Nanao's street. She trod quietly up to the house and peered through the window of the living room. A little light came from the back room where Nanao slept but she was not necessarily at home. Nanao would have left the light on even if she'd gone out. There was a mess of books and papers on the shelves and floor, no doubt some test or academic paper in progress. Runa rang the bell, hoping her sister would not be there. She wanted to let herself in, find the things she needed and turn straight back for the station. And when she did, she would run all the way.

Nanao opened the door, blinked. Runa found herself staring at her older sister, realizing that she would have to give an explanation. Seeing Nanao's expression, concerned and surprised, Runa wanted to tell her things she knew she could not. She sniffed a couple of times, kicked her foot casually against the doorstep.

"Hello, Nanao. It's been ages."

"Runa. What are you doing here?" Nanao's right hand moved up to her cheekbone, a gesture from childhood that always gave away her shyness in uncertain situations. Her perfectly straight eyebrows—just like Runa's—rarely betrayed her feelings, unless you knew her.

"I don't know." Runa stepped up into the doorway. "I just wanted to visit you."

"Of course. That's nice. Sorry, I wasn't expecting you. Come in then." She let Runa pass her, then went ahead to find slippers. "It's good to see you. You know you can come any time."

"I haven't seen you for months." Runa groped for something better. She should have thought of this before she arrived. She'd had two hours on the train and all she'd done was look out of the window at the darkness, having imaginary conversations with people she knew, trying to explain, to justify what she had done.

"There was a book I wanted to borrow, but I can't remember what it is now."

She put her feet into the cotton slippers, wriggled her toes inside them. Her shoulders were hunched and she felt weak. She stepped forward nervously and bumped into Nanao. Their arms touched and separated quickly.

"Runa, are you all right?"

"How's Hiroshi?"

"Fine. Still in Taipei, looking around factories."

"Of course. How's the university?"

"The same as ever. Well, no. Not quite the same, since I'm only teaching part time now."

"Why's that?"

Nanao looked at Runa as if she was stupid.

"The baby, Runa."

"Baby?"

"I'm pregnant. It's due in five months, in winter. And Hiroshi's away for another month at least, so I don't want to risk working too hard. I know I told you—"

How could Runa have forgotten? She had known about the baby for weeks. Even as she left the school building she'd been running names vaguely through her mind. But seeing Nanao looking no thicker than a sheet of paper, with circles under her eyes from working, it was hard to believe that anything was changing.

"You did tell me. I wasn't thinking."

"Come through and I'll get you a drink. I seem to spend the whole time writing exam papers. Still. How is school?"

Runa shrugged. She was about to say that it was fine but had already paused long enough for Nanao to know that something was wrong. She followed Nanao into the living room and knelt at the table. Nanao had switched the light on but there were trees outside the window and the room felt dark.

"How is it?" Nanao fixed her eyes on Runa.

Runa noticed specks of silver glittering in Nanao's hair and wondered how it could have got there. From paper, perhaps, or some kind of packaging. Surely Nanao would not have decorated her hair on purpose; she never wore a trace of make-up. Sometimes she didn't even brush her hair.

Runa tried to think. "I suppose nothing much has changed."

"You've traveled a hundred kilometers to borrow a book whose title you can't remember?"

"I'd love a drink." She wished she knew how to lie.

"There's some of Hiroshi's beer in the fridge. It's been there for ages. It needs drinking up."

"Yes, please."

Nanao stood to go to the kitchen.

"I'll do it, since I'm the guest." Runa overtook Nanao on the way into the kitchen and took a large bottle of beer from the fridge. She wasn't thinking about what she was doing and its cold wetness in her hand shocked her so that she almost let it slip through her fingers. Her legs wobbled and she felt hot as she grabbed for it.

"Where's the bottle opener?"

"In the drawer."

"Where are the glasses?"

Nanao sighed and appeared in the kitchen. "Let me."

They sipped from tall glasses. Runa peeped over the top of hers and wondered at her sister's solitary life in this little old house. The village was tiny and the university was miles away. Nanao didn't seem to know her neighbors. When Runa had asked about them in the past, Nanao simply shrugged and looked blank. Hiroshi spent more time away than at home and when he was there, he hardly spoke. He would come home from work late at night, watch game shows until the early hours of the morning. He was never rude; if you spoke to him he would answer but he never started a conversation, except with contestants on the television. So when he went away, it couldn't be much of a loss to Nanao. She never seemed to mind. But Runa would be lonely within five minutes if she were married to a man like Hiroshi. She would have to go out or bring people in.

"It's humid tonight."

"Did I wake you? Had you gone to bed?"

"No. I was getting some work done. To be honest I'm glad to have an excuse to stop. I've been working since I got up this morning and haven't accomplished anything yet. I found I'd made a mistake in one of the exam papers that affected everything else so I had to start again."

Sometimes Runa could not believe that she was Nanao's sister. Nanao the physicist, so hardworking, driven, responsible, married, and pregnant. She couldn't imagine her making a mistake. Nanao's glass caught her eye and she stared. The liquid lit was orange.

"You're not drinking beer? I just noticed."

"I'm pregnant, Runa."

"Oh, yes. Of course. You can't have alcohol now. That's a pity."

"You could look at it that way." Nanao ran a finger around the base of her glass.

"Never mind. I'll drink for you."

As they drank, Runa realized how tired she was. She had taken the bus from school at four o'clock and dashed to the train without eating. Not that she was hungry. She hadn't eaten much for days. She became more tired and more drunk and found she wanted to tell Nanao everything. How good it would feel to share the load. The secret kept fizzing up inside her and she was only just able to keep it in.

"So, what's happening at school?"

Nanao's voice was smooth and liquid. It reminded Runa of their mother's voice and it made her feel different, as if there were less of a hurry. Listening to that voice, she could almost doze off and sleep all night. So much had happened to her. She would tell Nanao a little of it, but not all. She spoke and her voice came out in a whisper.

"You know. It's not a perfect life. Everybody watches you all the time. It's not easy to do the things you want to, living in that village where there's nothing except the school." Nanao was listening intently. "And then, things happen."

"What things happen?" Nanao's voice lowered to match Runa's.

"Things. A lot of gossip."

"What kind of gossip?"

Runa couldn't stop. There was always part of her that wanted to break every promise she made to herself, or to anyone else for that matter—like snipping off all her hair every time she'd grown it to the length she wanted.

"You see, they're saying that a teacher has been having an affair with a pupil. One of the fifth years." She paused. "What do you think of that?"

Nanao didn't take her eyes off Runa.

"What do I think? Why are you asking me? I think it's wrong, of course. If it's true then I hope they've been found out and the teacher sacked."

"Mmmm. But it's not quite in the open yet. It was a secret

affair but someone took a photograph of the couple together. Now that person has written to one of them anonymously and is threatening to expose them. They can't tell anyone about it. Their lives will be ruined."

The air conditioner clanked into action and blew cool air across Runa's face. Nanao sat absolutely still. Runa knew she was working hard to hide her shock. Nanao was always calm. Amazement registered like the slightest ripple across a pond, then a moment of extra stillness as she adjusted. She opened her mouth slowly to speak.

"So in fact no one knows for sure apart from the teacher, the pupil, and the person, or people, with the photograph."

"It seems so."

"So then, Runa, this gossip is about you. Unless you're the anonymous writer."

"Of course I'm not. I would never do anything so under-hand."

Nanao folded her arms and looked out of the window as if she thought someone was out there. Runa knew it was possible. A person determined to ruin her life could have followed her here. Nanao turned her head back but didn't look at Runa.

"Are you still seeing him?"

"No. Not really."

"Not really?"

"I have to see him every day. I can't help it. He's there. It's not a serious relationship. If this letter hadn't come it would have blown over in no time."

"Tell me about him."

"There's nothing much to tell. I like him. He's very sweet

and good-looking. We were just attracted to each other. We have fun. I can't explain. It doesn't matter. It's going to happen sometimes, isn't it? Especially when there are so many bored people out in the middle of nowhere. Some teachers and pupils are bound to be close in age. I expect it's happened lot of times before."

Runa felt better. It was so reasonable when she said it aloud.

"That has nothing to do with it. It's wrong. I can't even be bothered to think about why. It just is. Runa, you are planning to go back there, aren't you? You're not running away?"

"I am going back." That was half true. "I just wanted to get away this evening."

"Is the picture absolutely incriminating? Is it not possible to make something up to explain the fact that you were together?"

Runa shook her head. "We were leaving a love hotel."

She pulled an envelope from her pocket and took out the photograph and letter. The picture showed a small building decorated like a fairy castle, flanked by a shoe shop and a hair salon. The two lovers were leaving, not touching but walking very close. Runa's face was visible and her lover's profile was clear. Their expressions were serious, guilty, almost comically so. There was a *mikan* tree right next to the hotel with ripe orange fruits hanging down. Runa noticed for the first time how nicely the tree framed the picture.

She realized that she must have intended to show Nanao the picture. Otherwise she would not have brought it. Sometimes she surprised herself.

"Of all the places to walk out of together. A love hotel. How are you going to explain that one away? How could you be so stupid?" Nanao threw the picture down. "It's indefensible."

"You don't understand, Nanao. I wasn't thinking about what anyone else was doing. We just went there to be alone together. It was what we both wanted and it made us happy. It wasn't any more serious than that. We didn't actually use the love hotel in the end."

"You changed your mind?" Nanao looked hopeful.

"No. All the rooms were full. It was a small one."

"At least you didn't use it."

"We went to others, on different occasions, but they were far away so I guess they were safer."

"Are you in love with him?"

"In love? No, I don't think so. What does that matter?"

Nanao seemed disappointed and Runa realized that if she had been in love with Jun then to Nanao that would have been a kind of justification. It would have been better. If love were involved the whole affair would have been understandable, but it wasn't. Love wasn't part of it.

"What shall I do?"

"You have to stop seeing him. Apart from that I think you should do nothing. The letter may just be something spiteful. Are they asking for money or anything?"

"No. They're saying they want to kill me."

"That's ridiculous. If your relationship ends immediately, perhaps they won't bother you again. But if any more comes of this you'll have to go and talk to the principal."

"There are only a few years between us. It's nothing. It's nobody else's business. If we'd met in a different situation—"

"Teachers and students can't date each other, Runa. You know that."

"It happens all the time."

"That's not the point. It's wrong."

"Wrong? What have I done wrong? I've been nice to him from the beginning. I've done everything right. The problem here is that someone is threatening me, that I can't be left alone to do what I want."

"Have you any idea who took the picture?"

"No."

"Who might have a grudge and not have the guts to say so?"

Runa fidgeted with the corner of the tablecloth.

Nanao rolled her eyes. "Is there anyone in particular?"

"Maybe an ex-boyfriend, I don't know. They get so jealous. You can't predict what they're going to do."

"You'll have to hope for the best. I can't believe you've got yourself into this. Don't you ever think about the consequences of your actions?"

"Sometimes I do and sometimes I don't." Her period was late, a consequence she refused to think about yet.

"You should calm down. One day you'll want to get married—"

"Married? Whatever for?"

Nanao looked exasperated, as if the answer was obvious. "If for no other reason than to allow me a rest from worrying about you."

"But if I was married, you'd have to worry about me a lot more."

Nanao laughed. "You're probably right."

"You know I am."

Runa looked around. She mustn't forget why she had come. "Can I stay here tonight?"

"Of course. It's too late for you to go home now. Sleep on it. We'll think about what to do in the morning. You've been irresponsible, but you're my sister and I will help you."

When Nanao had said goodnight and gone to bed, Runa waited for a few minutes. Then she searched the room in darkness looking for Nanao's passport. Nanao kept all her documents in one drawer and, sure enough, the passport was there. She took it and pressed it to the bottom of her bag. Nanao wouldn't know it had gone, not for months and then it wouldn't matter. Runa wrote a note for Nanao saying that she had decided to go back to the school and that she would call the next day, which was true.

She thought of the person, the letter writer who wanted to hurt her—who may have followed her—and it occurred to her that one more item could be useful. She went into the kitchen and looked through the drawers. She found a penknife—Hiroshi's perhaps—wrapped it in a cloth, put it into her bag, and slipped out of the house.

Goodnight, Nanao, she said in the blackness. She would head back to the school, but only for as long as it took to get a visa organized. A few days, a week at the most. In the meantime, there was just one more thing to do. She must call her friend. She had friends in many places, but no one would guess this one. No one knew about Ping.

Two

The girl wore a powder-blue uniform with a matching pillbox hat. She stood in the corner, cushioned by a circle of space. As she lifted her gloved hand to press the buttons on the panel, her mouth opened and a helium voice spilled out. The doors closed and the elevator went up. Her speech continued to the next floor where the elevator came to a gentle stop. She paused for breath and started on some new stream of words as a couple of passengers moved out into the ladies' shoe department. Perhaps she was thanking them for traveling with her. More customers stepped inside, turning abruptly silent as they crossed the threshold, and she bowed to each one, careful not to make eye contact. Her half-smile was constant.

Ralph removed his glasses, wiped the frames with a small cloth, replaced them. He was standing a pace behind, slightly to the side of her. He breathed in the scent of her hair. She smelled of the department store—clean, chic—as if she had sprayed a concentrate of the shop's scent into the air and stepped through it. He was a whole head taller so he had a perfect view of her polished black hair, her funny little hat. He didn't understand a word she said, but he stayed in the elevator at each new floor, listening to the garbled sound, breathing the pocket of air above her head. If he could just touch her, put his arm around the stiff blue cotton. Simply by being so close to him, she was calming his nerves.

He couldn't remember when he had last looked at a woman in this way. It was wonderful that he could do all these new things in Asia, starting here in Tokyo. At home he didn't bother to look because he knew what they were like, even the pretty ones. There was no mystery, no more secrets beneath the skin. He'd also noticed that younger women at home weren't always as clean as they might be. Now he was here, in this creepy, scary, sweetshop kind of place where he could have whatever he desired. And at midday today his life would be transformed. Until then, there was so much to see and enjoy, so much to prepare him for the change.

By the fifth floor, Ralph was the only customer in the elevator so the girl was talking and bowing for his pleasure alone. She must be aware of him, right there, aware that he was a man, that he was foreign. He wondered how his presence was affecting her, what ideas he might be putting into that head, slipping under the hat, that she couldn't show. For someone who spent her working days sliding up and down in a box, such moments would be her highlights, the stuff of daydreams and lunch-break conversations. He shifted slightly so that he was at her side. He tried to see her face but caught only a glimpse of pinkish cheekbone and the dusty outer edge of her eyebrow.

If he could just speak to her—but he never would. She narrated the journey to the sixth and seventh floors. For all Ralph knew, she could be saying *and by the way, you're so handsome.* On the eighth and final floor he walked through the doors. The girl held out an arm as if to show him the way. The gesture was all the more charming for the fact that there was only one way, and she was still reciting her piece. *By the way, I'd like to marry you.* He turned, watched the doors draw together like bedroom curtains, and the girl disappeared.

He looked around. It seemed he was not in the department store anymore but at the end of a little indoor street of restaurants and cafés. He had entered the store to buy a present and he wouldn't find one here. Now that he was up at the top of the building, he had nothing to do but go down again, and yet he couldn't. He didn't want to take one of the other elevators, but if he arrived back at the same elevator so soon, he'd look as though he didn't know where he was going. She'd think he was an idiot. He followed the shiny tiled floor and glanced into windows that contained models of food: tempura, sushi, spaghetti, pizza, sausages and scrambled egg on toast, glasses of green and pink liquid. It was late morning and people were already lining up for lunch. Ralph wasn't hungry and he shouldn't eat until he was ready to take his pills. And even if he wanted to try something, he wouldn't have the courage to order a meal. He didn't know how to eat the food and the people would stare.

He circuited the floor a couple of times, until the sight of plastic food began to turn his stomach, and returned to wait in front of the middle set of doors. *Open sesame,* he whispered, and they opened. She was there, moving her eyes from the panel to Ralph, so he saw her whole face. It was triangular and pale. Her smile lifted her cheeks. He wanted to smile back, but a crowd of young men piled in and shoved him to the rear wall of the lift. They were half his age, arrogant with hi-tech sneakers and loud voices. He could see nothing of the girl. On the ground floor, he walked out, took one look back, but already a fresh crowd was moving toward her. All that remained was a white gloved hand, sticking out among the pushing bodies, a high-pitched babbling voice, the tip of a hat.

But he must get a grip. There was so much to do and he was forgetting. He needed to find the gift. The store was more crowded now and he had no idea what would be right. Bright, shiny assistants were positioned at junctions in the aisles, welcoming customers. They shouted as he passed and made him jump; he wished they would go away. Buying a present was something he'd always wanted to be good at—to be able to express something of himself and the receiver in a single item—but what would do? Something feminine, edible, wearable? Something to show off to her friends?

There were stands and shelves of designer handkerchiefs, scarves, and bags. Colored silk and leather gleamed under the shop lights and hurt his eyes. There was jewelry too, but that would be expensive. Nothing seemed quite right for a person he had only spoken to once. A box of chocolates or a bunch of flowers would suffice but he'd like to go a little further. Ralph wanted to show some hint of himself, of his personality, in this gift. He should have brought a present from England, something from his own shop or one of his sketches, perhaps.

Three women pecked at a large red basket of hair accessories, pulling at objects, holding them up to each other, and making noises of excitement, approval, indecision. They were like geese around bread crusts. There were bows, clips, black and silver nets with small beads, colored combs with little spurts of black wig attached. Ralph was surprised. When he looked at women's hair, he never thought it might be fake. He wondered if such things were available in England, in shops he passed regularly. He wouldn't know. Women may wear things that were really no different from toupées, for all he knew. His own hair was thinning but he would never dare to stick on a bit of fake hair. Men just couldn't, not without the risk of ridicule. He wanted to take a closer look, to see how the things worked, but he was the only man in this section, the only foreigner in the shop, and it would seem strange. For a moment he stood still, confused.

He spotted a section selling men's ties and went to take a look. If he couldn't buy a present, at least he could afford a new tie. It would show the agency that he had made an effort, that he was smart and respectable, a man with expensive ties. They felt nice between his fingers, silky and cool. The one he chose was soft, maroon with a leafy design. He held it against his shirt and walked over to a mirror. The tie looked smart and classic but he was not sure what he looked like in it. He glanced at his reflection, turned sideways, took in his whole appearance, but was none the wiser. He looked anxious and hot, that was all. Mirrors rarely gave him much information. He peered into the glass but couldn't see himself—not that, like a vampire, he wasn't there—there just wasn't much of a face to see. He had two eyes, a pair of spectacles, a nose, a mouth, a chin, some hair. He saw them all but they never seemed to come together to make a recognizable face like the kind other people had.

A squirt of woody aftershave from the perfume counter made him feel clean, and he couldn't resist just one more trip in the elevator before heading for the station. He went up and down in each of the three elevators but the woman had gone and been replaced by different versions of her. Their uniforms smelled the same as hers but these girls were taller or shorter, their hair blacker or wavier. He was wasting time and now he would be late for his appointment. He went from the fourth to the ground floor and out of the store. This was no good. Why was he not concentrating on his appointment? He couldn't afford to be dreaming about any woman he happened to pass in a shop. He let himself get caught up like this, let people catch his eye and hold it, but there simply wasn't time anymore.

The building was tall and shabby. Stairs wound around the outside to the top, the ninth or tenth floor. Ralph put a thousand yen note and a couple of coins into the taxi driver's hand. For the first time, he didn't reach for his calculator to convert the fare into pounds. Whatever the cost, it was preferable to being lost or late. Sometimes you had to weigh things up. Besides, if he added the cost of the taxi to the price of his plane ticket and everything else, it was negligible. It was probably less than the airport tax. Or the cost of all the cups of coffee he'd had at airports. The taxi driver passed Ralph some change. Ralph put a few coins into his pocket and pressed the others back into the driver's hand as a tip. The driver seemed to think Ralph was confused about the change and handed it back again, counting the coins carefully into Ralph's palm the way you would count money to a child. Ralph's face turned hot and drops of sweat tickled his back. He stuffed the coins into his trouser pocket where they were heavy against his leg.

On the street he checked his watch. He was early. He sat on the bottom step to catch his breath. His feet were swelling and he loosened his shoelaces. He looked up and down the street, wheezing gently. There were smart boutiques, coffee shops, pleasant green trees. He liked the neat broad roads and junctions where pedestrians used the crossings and no one dodged dangerously between cars. People carried stylish paper shopping bags, walked with dainty footsteps. It was clean and orderly, if not beautiful. This could be a nice city—if only the heat and humidity didn't conspire to bring out all his ailments. If it were cooler he would spend more time exploring, more time sketching.

He had not bought a present and it was now too late. He pictured the two girls he had met the previous day—whatever their names were—how sweet they both looked in their little skirts, rose pink lipstick, long tidy hair. Unfortunately he had left the room before they did so he hadn't got to see them move. It would have been nice if they had given him a twirl before saying goodbye. Maybe he would ask them today—*would you walk a little for me? Just across the room, that's lovely*—and then he would decide.

He tried to recall the words he had read and reread in bed that morning. He couldn't remember them exactly but their gist was vivid.

Your Eastern Blossom will be beside you at all times, attentive and supportive. Her soft presence will be an asset to everything you do together. The Asian lady is gentle and caring. She understands her role as the nurturer and she will give you love and support without question because that is how she has been brought up in her traditional family environment. She does not resent it but loves to do her best to please you.

He wondered if it was all right to be sitting on the steps. He felt conspicuous; no one else was sitting on steps anywhere along the road. He couldn't shake off the fear that he might be doing something socially terrible or illegal. When you were abroad, you didn't know what they might arrest you for. In Singapore, he had heard, you couldn't even chew gum; not that he wanted to—too much chewing gum could cause stomach ulcers. After a few deep breaths it occurred to him that the girls might be looking down from a window. He wouldn't want to be seen so weakened, a crumpled old potato chip packet rustling around on the steps.

He climbed slowly to the top. The heat intensified with each step and the metal railing scorched his fingertips. Which of the girls would be waiting there for him? If both were there, how would he choose? And how would he know that he was right? There were no criteria. He could say, I find this one more attractive, that one more fun to be with, but you were never sure. He had made the wrong choice before. He looked up at the remaining concrete steps, chipped and uneven. Now that the time had arrived, he wished he were back home, cutting flowers in his garden, mowing the lawn in fine summer rain. He was suddenly nostalgic for the loneliness he was trying to escape, as if it had already gone. But it hadn't.

The agency reception area reminded Ralph of a botanical glasshouse. Large potted plants stood along each wall and in the corners. The air was humid, almost steamy, and water dripped somewhere in another room. Spidery ferns hung from the walls on either side of him. He sat back in his chair and leaves folded in front of his face so that he was peering through as if camouflaged. A fan near the desk began to whirr and Ralph let the air, though warm as blood, brush one cheek and then the other. Around the walls were crooked posters of Japanese women in kimonos. One woman was getting off a bus, another was cuddling a little dog. They were all pretty and charming, but they weren't quite straight and needed a good dusting.

Mr. K. popped up from behind the desk and exclaimed at seeing Ralph there.

"Mr. Turnpike. I'm so sorry. I didn't hear you come in."

He sat beside Ralph, pulled back the wisp of foliage that parted them and pushed it behind the back of the chair. He had a proper name—beginning with K and lasting for three or four syllables—but Ralph had forgotten it. It was no good with foreign words, hearing them only once and being expected to remember.

Mr. K. was stout and balding. Ralph looked at him and felt superior. Ralph may have been losing hair but was still slim, thinner in fact than perhaps he had ever been. Of course, they were not in competition. Mr. K. would be married already. He might have married when he was young so that his middle-age weight and shiny crown wouldn't matter at all. For Ralph, it all mattered still, but Mr. K. was Japanese so it was probably different. No doubt Mr. K. had never, ever had to cook for himself after a busy day at work.

Before leaving the UK, Ralph had forgotten that there would be Japanese men in Japan. He had somehow imagined a land of beautiful, mysterious women and then himself, so he wasn't sure how to talk to Mr. K. or how they would understand each other, culturally. When Ralph first came to the agency, he had expected to meet a British man. He'd thought it would be similar to the place in Bangkok where he'd found Apple several years before. That one was run by an ex-army officer called Tom. Ralph had half thought he would find Tom here in Tokyo, or at least some brother or cousin, showing him the ropes, discussing the different girls and introducing him to the nightlife. He was shocked when he met Mr. K. and realized that they would have to talk. Ralph needed to share with him all sorts of personal details. He knew what to expect of Japanese women—you could tell by looking at the pictures and there was plenty of reading material—but not a man.

He shifted on the chair to unstick his thighs from the fake leather.

"Mr. Turnpike. How are you today?" Mr. K.'s expression was one of assumed concern but perhaps he resented Ralph for his desirability to Japanese women and was hiding his feelings. It must be a difficult job. He would spend his working days in a state of envy, handing women over to tall Western men, each time silently affirming his own inferiority.

"I'm fine."

"You seem very hot. It's humid today, *ne*."

Mr. K.'s English was good but he tended to say *ne* at the end of his sentences. Ralph couldn't guess what it meant or whether Mr. K. knew he did it.

"Very hot, yes."

"Japanese summer is always hot and humid, *ne*." He stretched his arms.

"So I'm learning."

"Well. I expect you're wondering what response we have had from the ladies you met the other day."

"Yes. I would certainly like to know." Any moment now, he would be engaged. He should have brought a bottle of champagne. It would have been the perfect gesture.

"I'm sorry but—how can I say this?" His glance flickered between Ralph and the wall. "You need to keep all your options open in this situation."

"Yes. I am doing so. All my options are open." *Both of them*, he thought.

"Good. Because I think perhaps neither of the ladies is quite right for you."

"Oh." Ralph was thrown. "That wasn't my feeling at all." Ralph was thrown. His throat started clearing itself involuntarily. Surely Mr. K.'s opinion was not relevant. The girls could make up their own minds. "But I found the ladies delightful, both of them. We really hit it off. I know we only had a short meeting together, but there was something special between us. I could feel it. I don't quite understand what you're getting at."

"I mean, perhaps these particular ladies would not be the ones for you."

"You've just said that but I don't understand why. What did they say?"

"I'm afraid to tell you that neither of them has given a positive response."

Ralph's ears were ringing. The money he'd borrowed, his time away from the shop, and the expectations of the people he had told, all pressed down on him. He had planned to get married, had paid for everything. He thought he might stop breathing. *Steady on, Ralph. Deep breath.* Sweat dribbled down his chest and he couldn't move. He was melting and dripping like a candle.

Mr. K. went on. "But don't worry. We are here to help. If you want to come back tomorrow there are two other ladies to whom I would be delighted to introduce you."

"Oh, yes." Ralph heard his voice, gruff and pathetic. "Right-o. Of course. I'll come back."

"Mmmm. But, *ne*, there's a small point I should make. These women are from our C list. They are lovely ladies, I assure you, but they are a little older than the ones you have met so far. It's just that I feel you will have more success if you are prepared to meet ladies a little closer to your own age."

Ralph fingered his wrist. His pulse was racing. He must remember to take his pills as soon as he reached the hotel.

"I'm hardly ancient. I'm a little over forty."

"Yes, I know that but—"

"They're attracted to older men. I've heard it from lots of places and you must know it, too. It's a fact. It was the same in Thailand when I got my first wife."

"Yes, sometimes."

Ralph understood the problem. He looked older than he was, much older. In comparison, the girls looked younger than their stated ages. They probably thought he was lying. His father was grey and wrinkled at forty and Ralph had inherited all his father's bad genes.

"I don't see why you can't find me a younger woman. My first wife was very young indeed. She was nearly twenty years younger than me."

"Of course and I'm not at all surprised. Mmmm." He paused. Ralph wondered what this *mmmm* meant. "Your previous wife, Mr. Turnpike, she is now . . .?"

Ralph mopped his face with a sodden handkerchief. He shouldn't have mentioned Apple. He hadn't meant to do that at all. This had nothing to do with her. She was maneuvering her way back into his head and he must put an end to her before she injured him again. He must replace her with a new wife as soon as he could.

"She's gone. All right. I'll come tomorrow. Just to get my money's worth. And to show good manners to these ladies."

"That's a very wise decision, Mr. Turnpike. I'm certain you won't regret it. And if any more of our A- or B- list women express an interest, I'll be sure to have them here tomorrow, too. We won't waste any opportunity to help you, *ne*. Do you play golf?"

"No. Why?" Ralph had never liked sport. He knew he could

try, but he didn't like the people who liked sport. He preferred to keep fit by walking on gentle hills, with his sketchpad, sometimes with his half-brother or one of his fellow drinkers from the Happy Man. He would play table tennis or snooker if it was there but that was his limit. Members of his local golf club were high on the list of people he didn't much like. They had their small businesses—as he did—and then their flowery wives and dull, dull conversations about second homes and school fees.

"Personally I find it a pleasant way to relax when I'm stressed."

"I've never played."

"Is your hotel good?"

"It's all right. The best I can afford." He would prefer not to share with Mr. K. the details of his trip.

"Swimming pool?"

"A very small one." Ralph had spotted it from the hotel elevator but hadn't thought of going in. He couldn't stand communal changing rooms and wasn't good with chlorinated water.

"Perhaps a swim or two before tomorrow would help prepare you, ne. You know, exercise can be a form of meditation. I just mean that you mustn't take all this so seriously that you make yourself unwell. If you're not used to Japanese heat, you must take extra care of your health. You seem rather hot."

"Don't worry. I'll be fine."

"I'm sure you will. I look forward to seeing you again."

The door swung shut and Ralph was on the staircase, dizzy above the street. He was C list. He wondered if there was a D or an E list. He suspected that he had already reached the bottom. This place was bad for his heart, bad for his blood pressure.

If he concentrated, he could hear his blood agitating through his veins, feel his feet inflating like balloons and pushing against the hot leather of his shoes. The pavement back to the hotel was soft in the heat. It felt spongy. He could imagine he was walking on gingerbread and that nothing around him was real.

Three

The pupils were practicing for the annual English speech contest. They sweated boredom in their rows and batted steamy air from desk to desk with paper fans. The selected competitors came forward one by one and droned through their pieces. One of the prettier girls had a hand mirror propped against her pencil case and was tilting her head from side to side to get the best view of her lips, perhaps to check her lipgloss or practice her pout. The classroom windows were open and voices from outside drifted in. Two geography teachers, in different rooms, were explaining the same point about rubber plantations in Malaysia. Their voices mingled, then alternated as if one were the interpreter for the other, though they were speaking the same language. Out on the field, Mr. Kawasaki screamed at a boy for daring to come to baseball practice with a sprained wrist.

Runa was facing her class, her chalk box and register on the window sill beside her. She must concentrate on the speeches, give comments and criticism at the end, correct pronunciation and persuade the pupils to add a little intonation, even if it was incorrect, but they were sending her to sleep. She looked out at the school grounds, the boys playing softball with energy that was hard to believe on such a hot day. Her eyes moved to the edge of the playing field, to the bamboo forest that circled the school, the lumpy green mountains beyond. Soon she would be hundreds of miles away.

Almost a week had passed since she'd returned from Nanao's flat and she hadn't slept through a single night. She had tossed, turned, sweated, and boiled in her bed. She had crept out into the forest and breathed woody air for hours, had taken scalding baths and showers that lasted all night. She had scoured the area around her to see if someone was following, but there was never a sign. She hadn't closed her eyes and slept. And her dreams had come while she was awake. And still her period hadn't started. But Nanao's passport had arrived back from the Chinese consulate that morning, stamped with a tourist visa. Runa was equipped for her journey and would leave after dark when it was safe to get away.

Her stomach was in knots. Jun Ikeda was watching her closely from his desk by the window, but did he know about the letter or the photograph? Did he think that this was just a regular school day? Certainly he could have no idea of her plans and she must tell him soon. But how would she explain anything to Jun when she couldn't even look at him? Runa let her eyes move around the room, taking in all the other pupils.

Looking out at the faces she realized that she would miss them. It was so completely Jun's class that she hadn't given

much thought to the others and now she was sorry. A couple of
boys were folding their arms on their desks, ready to drop their
heads and snooze as soon as they knew the next speech had
begun. Ties were loose, socks were rolled down to the ankles,
and every now and then some spiritless voice would murmur,
it's hot, it's hot. Even the most dedicated students were taking
little notice of the speakers, but were reading through their
own speeches, rehearsing silently at their desks.

A shrill voice pierced the thick air. Runa looked up at the
platform and saw an earnest, bespectacled sixteen-year-old girl
reading from the paper in her hands. *And I think the world would
be a happier place if we all remembered to do this every day*, she
shrieked. *That's all*. And she stepped down, to feeble applause
from her two or three best friends.

"Thank you," Runa said. "Who's next?"

She should be concentrating, last day or not. She must not
arouse suspicion. Among the titles listed on the board were *Always Reach for Your Dream*, *The Importance of a Smile for Human
Beings*, *Things I Have Learned from My Grandmother*. Runa's
favorite was *What We Can All Learn From Growing a Pumpkin*,
though she was not sure she cared to know the answer. She
couldn't believe that it would be much help today.

She walked to the back of the room, tried to imagine she was
Jun Ikeda watching his favorite teacher moving around at the
front. She saw herself stretch up to write on the board, lean
over desks to solve problems, toss her hair lightly when she
turned to answer a question in a different part of the room. She
laughed at their jokes, helped them with the harder aspects of
English pronunciation.

She looked at the space in front of the blackboard and the image of herself was clearer than if she were looking in a mirror. It was not difficult to see through Jun's eyes. She understood Jun's way of absorbing her. She knew how he looked at her. He thought she was beautiful, incredible. He thought that every part of her was something special.

Runa found herself smiling at the small girl who had just arrived on the platform. Her hair was in two high bunches with little green bows. This was against the school rules; they could have two braids but only one ponytail and no ribbons. But the girl had a sweet and honest face so everyone knew that even the principal would let her pass in the corridor without comment. The girl was in the cheerleading club, the Cheer Girls, and Runa had seen her sometimes, standing at the top of human pyramids behind the school, somersaulting through the air with her yellow pom-poms flying like dandelion heads. The girl smiled back at Runa as she recited. Runa tuned in to listen to the speech and realized that it was about to finish.

For the remainder of the lesson she focused. She was not sure how to advise the speakers, since they seemed to know more than she did. She admired their certainty, their sweeping ability to make the world right and keep it simple. We must reach for a dream because we can't live happily without a sense of achievement. We should smile because it will make other people smile and then we'll all be happy. Grandmother lived to be a hundred and two and she never got up after six o'clock in the morning and she ate a fish every day for breakfast.

What I learned from growing a pumpkin is that some things are

*difficult and they die if you get it wrong. But you can always try
again next year.*

Runa wanted to tell them they were ridiculous, nonsensical,
but she didn't. She nodded encouragement. Between speeches
she corrected their pronunciation, made them practice *th*, *l* and
r. She smiled as she talked—she couldn't help it—and they
frowned in concentration, repeating the words and sentences
to themselves. In her sleeplessness she wondered if perhaps
they were right and it was indeed so simple. You could brush
away all the problems of the world with a heartfelt platitude.

And then, what she wanted and feared the most: Jun Ikeda
hauled himself to the front, stepped onto the platform. She felt
acutely self-conscious but was not sure whether for herself or for
him. He was handsome in his uniform, easily the best in the
school. The sun glinted on his hair, showing a glow of red, and
she wondered if he had been dyeing it. She would have liked to
go forward and touch it, push back the strand that had fallen
over his forehead, as she did after sex, when his face shone with
sweat and his hair clung to his skin. Knowing she could do
nothing intensified the desire. All the hiding, the pretending
there was nothing illuminated and heightened what there was.
Yes, yes, Nanao, she said inside her head, *I know it is wrong.* Of
course she knew—just by looking around at the other pupils
who needed her to belong to them too. She saw that she had a
role to play and rules to follow. But at moments like this she
knew who she was. She wouldn't want to live without them.

Jun began to speak and she smiled to herself, ran her finger
along a scratch in the desk. He was reading badly on purpose,
his pronunciation all Japanese, his tone flat and bored. He was

embarrassed to be good in front of her with his friends watching. Being successful at school had nothing to do with pleasing teachers; she knew that. His speech was a standard piece about teamwork in basketball. The text was not bad but he would not win any prizes for such a mumbled performance. And she knew how good he could be. She had spent a night in a tiny karaoke room with him and no one else, and she had heard him sing English love songs with perfect pronunciation. She knew what he could do.

Her mind wandered off again, to the last time they met, over a week before and she let herself half doze through the memory.

That night they had climbed onto the school roof. They stood directly above Jun's classroom. They had been walking through the woods, and when they emerged, Jun threw his arms wide and said that he wanted to climb a mountain. None of the mountains in the region was close enough to reach without a car, so Runa led him up the fire escape, through a door and out onto the rooftop. No one will know, she told him. See how high we are.

And Jun said, we've conquered the school, we're turning it inside out, into something else. Runa was already in her underwear—white and silky—dancing around the edges of the roof. He told her to be careful and Runa said, no, I don't want to be. She laughed and waved her arms around. I'd rather jump than be careful, she said. Jun was standing right in the middle, swinging his arms gently through the space. We could meet each other in the middle of the day up here, if no one was watching the fire escape and then we could be together even at school. Runa walked to him. No, she said, people would see us if they were on the field. Not if we were lying down, he replied and kissed her neck. We could smoke up here and everything. Runa laughed at Jun's sweetness and he blushed. Then they heard a voice from below. They peered over the edge and saw an old woman passing in front of the school gates. She was calling, who's there? Who's there? Runa said, she's probably demented. Jun knelt between her legs, stroked her thighs, kissing her through the silk. Maybe, he said when he emerged, she heard us talking but didn't think to look up here. Who would?

It was exciting, once, to think they might have been caught. But now the idea made Runa sick.

She knew that as he stood in front of his classmates, talking about the pleasure of belonging to the basketball team, he was thinking of her. Her eyes were burning into him like torches, and she knew he felt the glare.

He looked up and met her gaze. He had finished speaking. His head was bent forward as though he could only face her from a slight angle. She looked back steadily and spoke in her projected, teacher's voice, giving basic advice on how to improve, and he took it with surly nods. Did he resent her, his girlfriend, talking to him like this, or was she just a teacher now? Perhaps he was as aroused as she was by this polarizing of their roles. Really, his speech was so bad that she should have made him do it again but that would be cruel. She wrote a note, a dangerous note, and handed it to him. "Practice these points and you'll be fine," she said. *Tonight*, she had written.

The electronic bell chimed to end the lesson. The class leader shouted for everyone to stand and bow. Chairs scraped.

The twenty-four boys and twenty-three girls gave a perfunctory dip of the head. Runa nodded back and left the room.

She headed upstairs for the teachers' room, saying good morning to teenagers and staff all the way. She flopped down at her desk, slid forward on her clunky swivel chair, and waited for the midmorning meeting to begin.

The principal made various announcements about weekly, monthly, and special tests, also about building giant structures for the school festival next term. Runa's classroom was to become the ballroom of the *Titanic* for the weekend. She wrote down what he said, to show that it mattered to her, to show that she was not planning to run away long before the school festival.

The principal paused to take a deep and dramatic breath. Every gesture, every sound that came from him, seemed rehearsed for the stage, as if, after years as a high-school principal, he couldn't communicate in any other way. Runa had once taken time off work with flu and when she returned, the principal asked after her. He barked his concern as if she were a class of forty-five delinquents. Today's performance—the long inhalation and half-closed eyes—said that he was shocked and appalled, and by someone present. There were squeaks from all around the room as the teachers swung round on their chairs to see. He clutched a piece of paper in his right hand and stared at the staff with gravity. He said that he had one more announcement. The knot in Runa's stomach pulled tighter. She wrapped her arms around her abdomen and pressed hard.

He had received a letter informing him that somewhere there was a photograph of a teacher and a pupil leaving a love hotel. He had not seen the photograph so couldn't know whether or not it existed. If it were true, he said to the gathering, the man must tell him immediately. As a private school with a formidable reputation, such a scandal would not be tolerated. If the girl's parents found out, it would be a disaster. He, personally, would do his best to ensure that the teacher in question never worked again.

Kawasaki, who sat behind Runa, whispered to another colleague, "I heard that the teacher is female. But that's hard to believe, don't you think?"

Runa and Kawasaki had had a fling a few months before and she was glad to hear that he didn't suspect her.

The other teacher grunted in surprise and the conversation ended.

Runa filled in her registers, keeping her back to him, hunched over her desk. This was bad news though she was finding it hard to stay awake. She knew she must be alert now but her eyes kept closing. There was a jar on her desk containing a water lily. A first-year girl had presented it to her the previous week for no special reason. Runa was so happy at the time that she felt proud to be a teacher and, for a few moments, forgot her usual feeling of being a fraud. For almost a whole day she had believed that teaching was her vocation. Her head nodded forward with sleep and her hair brushed the glass jar. She jumped up quickly. For now she was safe—the principal thought she was a man—but she had little time. That night she must call Ping and tell her to have a bed ready.

*   *   *

The school was burning up in the midday heat. The windows along every corridor were open and a weak breeze blew through. A couple of boys had stopped by the drinking fountain in the stairwell and were soaking their handkerchiefs to squeeze over their necks. They laughed with pleasure as cold drops of water slid under their collars. They were small, first-years probably, twelve-year-olds who were safe to teach because they were quite clearly children, could not be otherwise if they tried. It was lunchtime and Runa must find Jun Ikeda, tell him that his life was about to change, that there was no point in meeting tonight because she was about to disappear.

Navy uniforms filled the staircases, flowed into the hall and burst out through the main doors like flood water. Runa stood still and let them rush past. Any one of these children could have known about her and taken the picture, but she would hate that most of all. She would have preferred the anonymous schemer to be another teacher, or some nosy person in the village with no connection to the school, even a member of Jun's family.

The sun scorched the dirt sports field, turning it from brown to orange. Runa hovered on the edge, wiped sweat from her fingers and forehead with a handkerchief as she looked across. Jun was in front of the gym building with a few other boys. Taller than his friends, muscular and deeply tanned, he twisted a basketball around in his hands. She walked toward the group, as if heading for the door to the gym, and tried to catch his eye. He ignored her. They had both become used to not-seeing, but she had to tell him. He may know nothing of the letter and photograph, the impending scandal. *Look at me*, she wanted to scream. *Don't you want to know what I've done to you? There's no point in ignoring me now. We've been found out. We're not having a secret affair anymore. It's over and it's known. Look at me.*

A small gust of wind cooled the playing field and the air seemed to bump between them. One of Jun's friends said something and the group laughed, a teenage boy laugh that Runa recognized from the classroom; as soon as each one realized that the others had joined in, he laughed harder still, a laughter of reassurance as much as of humor. It was so different from the giggles and shrieks of the girls. With the girls, you would never know if one were being murdered.

And she saw Jun now as he was, just a kid with his friends, probably thinking about his homework for the next class. Somehow, mixed up with those thoughts, would be Runa and tonight's meeting. She couldn't imagine how they fitted together in his head, but she knew he was excited about tonight and had no idea that anything might be wrong. It was painful. The thought that she could be pregnant with his child horrified her. Why had she never seen how young he was?

So she would not tell him then. It would do no good. When she had gone it would be up to him to decide whether to admit or deny the affair. And no one would blame him. It was Runa they would want to find. She went back into the school, closed the door behind her, knew it was the last time she would do so.

A boy with a broom in his hand was sweeping around the teachers' shoe lockers. As Runa changed slowly from her outdoor shoes back into her sneakers, she realized he was staring at her. He had spoken and was waiting for an answer.

"So is it today then?" He stopped sweeping and put the broom behind him, as though out of politeness.

"What's that?"

"The test. Teacher, are you all right?"

"Yes, fine. A test. Did I say it would be today? Then I think it must be."

She had no memory of writing a test. She wondered if she should have. She would check her desk and see if she'd written anything before she went to Nanao's house. She knew the boy's face but was too tired to remember which class, or even which year, he belonged to. If she was lucky, the test would be some general thing that had already been written by the head of English. She was beginning not to care.

The last class finished with yawns and a tired bow. Runa slipped out of the classroom before the pupils had time to come at her with the inevitable questions and chatter. In an alcove of the teachers' room used for photocopying and gossip, the principal's voice was a harsh stage whisper; now he was expressing frustration, martyrdom. Runa glanced across. He was hissing about something with Mr. Araki, the music teacher, and Mr. Araki was trying to get the principal into a store cupboard for privacy. The principal pushed past him and stormed away. Another teacher joined Araki to find out what had happened. Runa picked up a book and hovered out of sight near the photocopier, pretended to be finding a page. She listened to the conversation.

"What's the latest?"

"It was a newspaper reporter, on the phone to him."

"How can he be sure? It could be the letter writer pretend-ing."

"Well, he can't be sure. But he says he has no choice but to believe it. And the person gave a name so I suppose he could check."

"And the reporter knows who it is?"

"No names, but he has seen a copy of the photograph."

"Good grief. How many do you think are in circulation?"

"It's hard to guess. But the teacher is a woman and the stu-dent is a boy. And that's not all. The reporter says he also has evidence of immorality and under-age drinking in a local bar, encouraged by the very same woman."

"That's nonsense. There are only half a dozen female teach-ers here anyway and as far as I can see, they stay in every night. Though, now I think about it, someone does come to mind. Even so, an affair with a boy . . ."

They shook their heads, lowered their voices, until Runa couldn't tell whether they were still speaking.

Later, in the hallway of the teachers' apartments, the gossip continued. This was going to be a big story, they said. Ever since the arson attack on a school in the next city where the perpetrators were a gang of teenage girls and boys, the papers had been obsessed with the region's declining moral standards, especially in schools, especially crimes committed by women.

Kawasaki passed Runa in the corridor. "I don't think it's even true. But if it were, and I knew the woman, I'd wring her neck."

Runa dressed in the night, packed a bag of clothes. There was nothing she could do about Jun and there was not time to call

Ping. She took Nanao's passport and the knife and slipped out of her apartment into the darkness of the bamboo forest. Among the trees a tall figure moved toward her. She stopped breathing and tried to keep still but clearly he had seen her. And as he came closer, she recognized his silhouette, tall and athletic. It was Jun. She dropped the bag, kicked it into the undergrowth, and stepped forward.

"I'm early," he said. "It would have been difficult to get out of the house later. My dad sometimes comes home from work really late so now he'll just think I've gone to bed already. But, anyway, you're early, too."

He was wearing jeans, sneakers, a yellow T-shirt. His hair was gelled and combed immaculately. He looked to Runa like a picture from a teen magazine. She put her fingertips gently on his chest then pressed her whole hand to feel his basketball player's muscles. She had hoped to escape before he arrived but couldn't help feeling happy to see him and touch him once more.

"I'm glad you came. But we can't stay long tonight."

"I don't mind. Whatever you want. Let's go on the roof again." He kissed the soft skin on her inner arm, the way she had taught him, the way she liked it.

"I don't think it's such a good idea tonight. Someone might see. You know, the teachers' apartments are so near, and our voices could be heard."

"It doesn't matter. Nobody knows a thing about us or even suspects."

He was so beautifully happy, so straightforward, and she couldn't bear to tell him. So she followed him up the rusty stairs, watching his feet jump two steps at a time. She was tired as she shuffled out onto the roof. She should have been halfway to the next village by now. She walked to the center, stood still with her arms folded across her chest. The air was still warm and close though there was a strong breeze up there above the trees. The sky was murky, just one or two stars showing.

"You're in a funny mood tonight." He stood behind, put his arms around her, and drew her close. She rubbed her face against his bare arm, felt the soft hairs. Their skin was damp with sweat and, briefly, they stuck to each other. He rocked her from side to side. "What's the matter?"

"Nothing." She turned, smoothed his hair, rubbed her nose against his. "Nothing at all."

"It's because of my speech practice today, isn't it? You thought I was terrible. I was and I know it. I'm sorry. It's just that I can't do that kind of thing in front of you."

"I know."

"It's embarrassing, with all my friends there. Even though they know nothing—I can't explain." She loved his eyes at moments like this. They were big and limpid, so uncertain. She wanted to take his hand and lead him through each piece of his life.

"I understand. Jun, that's why I'm worried about seeing you anymore."

His head jerked back, as if his whole face had just woken up.

"No. No, please. It doesn't matter that much. I don't want to win the stupid contest anyway. It's the least important thing in my life. Why would I want to win a speech contest? I don't even want to enter it at all. You're far more important to me."

Her chance to say goodbye was slipping through her fingers and she couldn't stop it.

"All right. Perhaps I could try and have my timetable altered so that I'm not teaching you anymore. They might let me do that." She considered the idea, almost believing that it would happen. "I'd have to come up with a plausible reason though."

"I like being in your class. It's the only reason I keep coming to school." He walked to the edge of the roof and lowered himself carefully until he was sitting with his legs dangling over the side. He was quiet for a few moments, then spoke in a daydream voice. "I like to be high up. It suits me. I'd rather be looking down on the world than be a part of it, worrying about someone looking down on me."

"Jun, that's dangerous." But she went and sat beside him, experienced a pleasant dizziness when she looked down on the school, the gym, the playing field, the bike sheds. During the day the buildings acted out being a school. At night, everything reverted to its normal state and time moved forward.

"Runa-teacher, we'll have to come up here in winter."

"Why's that?"

"Because of the snow." He gesticulated vaguely toward the trees. "When it lands on the bamboo and makes it lean over, we'll get the best view of all." He was swinging his legs, looking at the trees, even now anticipating the winter scene.

Runa remembered the snow from last year, how the bamboo sprang back into shape as it began to melt. But it never happened when you were looking. If you hung around for long enough, you might hear a low creaking but then you'd turn to see which tree it was and behind you snow would thud to the ground and another tree was upright again.

"Hey, do you want to hear something funny?" Jun was chuckling. "My parents suspect that I've got a girlfriend. I heard them talking. They say they can tell from my behavior, though I don't know what they mean by that. They're very excited."

"They know? That's terrible." Runa wondered if they had seen the letter or the photograph.

"It's all right. No, in fact it's good. They're relieved to discover that there are girls who like me so it doesn't matter that I come and go a bit. Of course, they will never think that my girlfriend is my teacher."

She put her hand behind his head, pulled him forward to kiss him. Already his kisses, his words, were becoming more remembered than real. She rested her fingers on his shoulders, somehow the most solid part of him, to convince herself that he was there, to stop him falling too quickly into the past.

"I'm sure they don't know that I'm often out all night."

"But they would mind, if they knew."

"As long as it's not before an exam I don't think the world would end. And after that I'll be at university and it won't matter. You'll leave the school, too, and become a famous actress or model. Or you'll be managing your own bar and I'll come and help you serve the customers."

Runa laughed. "You're good at looking at the future. It's something I've never been able to do. But you might not be so keen on me when I'm not your teacher anymore."

"What are you talking about? I'd feel the same if you were a plumber, or anything, if you were married with five children. I mean, it's not just because I'm a student that you like me, is it?"

Runa shook her head, rested her cheek against his. "Of course not." But even as she felt his skin, began to kiss it, she wondered if she was telling the truth.

"Runa-teacher, shall we go to the Octopus? I want to sing." He was playing with her fingers, squeezing them one by one. "I want to sing love songs again."

"We can't, not tonight. I'm . . . I don't feel like it." And she didn't have time. She looked out at the mountains. She must go soon and without hurting Jun.

"But it'll help me with my English pronunciation." He looked more closely at her. "Something's really wrong, isn't it."

"No. I'm just tired."

"Of course. I'm sorry. You work hard at school and you need to sleep. Why don't we meet tomorrow and go to the Octopus?"

"Yes. That would be good. We'll go tomorrow. We'll sing all night and come here afterwards to drink. And if the sky is clear, we'll watch the stars. We'll have the perfect night together."

"Thank you. And I promise you, I'll practice and practice my speech until it's perfect. I won't let you be ashamed of me."

They kissed, quickly, because Jun was already impatient for the next day. He hurtled down the fire escape ahead of Runa. Before running off into the woods, he planted a kiss on her forehead. She waited until she was sure that he had gone, then touched the spot, the exact place where his lips had been. She picked a leaf from the ground, blew gently on it to remove flecks of soil, wiped the kiss away. There was no point in holding onto anything now, and a kiss was evidence of the crime.

Four

Ralph took a cold bath at the hotel. He didn't dry himself but dripped water through to the bedroom, lay naked on the bed and enjoyed the new sensation of shivering. He opened his catalog, *Eastern Blossoms*, at a random page.

They are not spoiled by exposure to Western culture or women's lib. They are pure, protected by their traditions and families. Any man that can marry one is VERY LUCKY.

The person who wrote that hadn't met Apple. She was traditional, beautiful, on the outside. Then he'd got her to England and she turned sour. Sour Apple. And he couldn't blame the agency. Her performance had been flawless. Hadn't Ralph himself been taken in by her beguiling innocence? At the memory of meeting Apple he made a feeble attempt at masturbation. But the creeping heat started to return, and the exertion put a sharp pressure on the inside of his skull, so he stopped and kicked *Eastern Blossoms* off the bed. He would wait until the night when it was cooler. At the moment he felt pathetic, ridiculous. His temper was simmering and for no good reason.

The day had begun perfectly and that made him more annoyed, as if he had brought this on himself by hoping for too much. He had been excited about his appointment and woke early, had a cup of coffee—which he was supposed to avoid—in the hotel restaurant. The silly buzz of anticipation gave him the confidence to go outside and explore. He took his sketchbook with him to create a memento of his visit. He went for a long walk, took a couple of trains. He found a nice park and sketched some pine trees and a temple. He managed to work a vending machine and get a can of lemonade. But—see?—it was a mistake. He should have stayed at the hotel and thought about what to do if the girls didn't want to meet him again, then gone directly to the agency. Instead he had gone to the department store and let himself be captivated by some anonymous girl. Such dreamy optimism was asking for trouble.

He was reaching a decision. He would give the Japanese agency one more chance. The girls he had met were good, there was no denying. He recalled their anxious smiles as they shook his hand. No, they hadn't given any sign that his age was a problem. They were perfectly charming and he would happily have arranged a second meeting with either. He was sure that they had liked him, too. After all, they both smiled through the interviews, answered all his questions and giggled at his jokes. Mr. K. was just jealous. It was far more likely that they were nervous about moving abroad and leaving their families. Or that their families opposed the match and didn't want them to leave the country with a man they hadn't had a chance to size up. Or it may have been that England was not the place they wanted to live. He had heard that young Japanese people were very interested in America.

He would return and see what else they had to offer, what exactly was on the C list. Until then, he couldn't bear to spend another night alone in the hotel. He took a list of phone numbers from his travel wallet and dialed the last one. All this travel, the reawakening of Apple and memories of Thailand, made him long for that heady, multicolored, coconut-flavored, anything-was-possible atmosphere of Bangkok. He wanted to recapture it and live through that time again.

A voice answered and said something in Japanese that sounded like *washingmachine*.

"Hello. Is Terry there?"

"Yes, Terry speaking." An English accent, at last. Ralph held the receiver against his head with both hands, felt he could cry.

"This is Ralph Turnpike. Jed's friend from the Happy Man. You might remember me. We met in Thailand one evening a few years ago. I'm in Japan."

"Oh, yes. Jed mentioned you were coming. We went for a meal in Bangkok, right? There was a group of you."

"And to a cabaret."

"Did we? Probably. I don't remember too much to be honest. I think I was drunk for most of that holiday. You're here on business?"

"Business. Yes, sort of. Just a couple of weeks. I wondered if you wouldn't mind a drink one evening, if you're not too busy."

"Why not? I'm pretty tied up later this week but—"

He was being brushed off, again. Twice in one day. "Oh, never mind then. It was just a thought."

"No, no. I was going to say, how about tonight? It's short notice, I know. I suppose you're doing all the formal entertainment stuff with your company. Are they giving you much time to yourself while you're here?"

"A bit. I don't think I've got anything planned for tonight. Jed mentioned that you know the nightlife here pretty well."

"I've lived here a while. You want to go to a bar tonight? We could do that."

"I might as well get a little of the local flavor. When in Rome and all that."

"I'll think of somewhere and call you back."

"If you have any other friends who might . . ." How to say, *please bring some pretty girls?*

"I'll see if anyone's around."

"So, you live in Japan all the time? You work here?"

"That's right. I'll call you back."

"Right-o then. I'll wait by the phone."

Ralph stretched on the bed. He wanted to go outside again, start the day from scratch as if he were just waking up, at nightfall. What he had in Bangkok, he could find again in Tokyo.

He had lost his virginity in his early twenties, but the break that followed was almost long enough to see its restoration. So in Bangkok Jed had helped him to arrange a refresher with a couple of prostitutes. In a darkened room, two creatures as supple and supernatural as black cats teased, probed, and licked him to a state of joy. He had cried out in the night, as if howling for some lost person, and afterward he'd cried into his pillow. In the morning the sun rose slowly and, feeling as if he had penetrated the whole universe, he visited an orchid farm. He wanted to fill his head with exuberant color. There were orchids of every hue, but now he could only remember the purple ones. Later he went into a shop and bought meters of silk, to give to the next woman he slept with, who—he decided that day—would be his wife.

Now he liked to roll the pieces of memory together so that he met the women in beds of purple orchids, with people walking past not watching, but knowing he was there. And the women were wrapped up in lengths of silk that he unraveled gently.

Satiated with sex and sex shows, Jed, Terry, and the others had headed south for snorkeling and Ralph said he would take a train to Chiang Mai and join a trek. It was a good story; everyone knew he liked mountains and cooler air. Instead, he stayed in Bangkok, visited an agency, and found Apple.

And Bangkok really was a magical place because, when he took the beautiful Apple away from it, she sort of shriveled into nothing. All her sweetness evaporated until there was nothing left that was nice. In England she was cruel, taunting, uninteresting, and altogether bad. It was a dreadful time. And when it ended he told people that she had left him and returned to Thailand. They believed him and so he believed himself. It did appear to be true. There were no knocks at the door, no news reports or difficult questions. No one in Thailand wrote or called to ask after her; she'd just gone. He was able to think of her, happily back in Thailand with her family, chasing butterflies or walking under palm trees. And since nothing bad had happened since, he was sure that Apple had forgiven him.

                            *   *   *

Terry was at least six feet tall, bigger than Ralph. His mouth,
nose, ears, bulging eyelids were all huge. Every feature was as
solid and tense as a clenched fist. When he smiled though, he
softened. His handshake was short and warm. He led Ralph from
train to train and then along a noisy crowded street. The sun had
gone down but the air was still wet and hard to breathe. There
were so many people going this way and that with such speed and
purpose Ralph felt he was walking through a huge factory where
the walls and roof were miles away and the noise of production
never stopped. Most of the people they passed were in their teens
or twenties, out in groups for a night of fun. Not one of them
glanced at the two foreign men. Ralph was a little disappointed.

On the way to the bar they stopped at a bank so that Ralph
could get some cash on his credit card. Terry pressed the buttons
on the machine and looked away as Ralph tapped in his secret
number. A little blonde woman appeared on the screen, bowing
with a wide smile as the machine dispensed Ralph's money. He
blinked.

"Crikey. That's something you don't get at home."

"There's another button you can press. It makes the woman
turn round the other way so you can see up her skirt."

"Is there?" Ralph glanced at the panel of numbers.

Terry was looking at him with amusement.

"Joke."

"Oh. Ha ha. I get it."

How was he supposed to know what there was and what
there wasn't? On a lamp post near him was a poster with a car-
toon girl in a skimpy bikini, legs wide open, smiling enticingly.

Around it were colorful stickers of half-naked women and a variety of phone numbers. They were everywhere. Why not on the bank machine too?

As they walked, Terry talked about his day at the magazine where he worked and explained that he had interviewed a famous *shamisen* player for an article about traditional Japan.

"Traditional Japan. That's what I'm interested in," said Ralph. "The delicate things, the old ways of living life. We've lost so much of that in England. We don't know what our traditions are anymore."

"Do you know much about Japanese music, then? To be honest, I really don't, so I had to bluff my way through the questions. Luckily the old boy went on at great length regardless of what I said."

"No, I don't know much. I meant, in general. I like traditional things, especially women." He laughed, hoping to get a response from Terry.

"I'm interested in Japanese poetry. I'm actually a poet as well as a journalist. Let's go in here."

Terry seemed more intellectual, a bit more respectable than Ralph remembered him. And smug, as if Ralph was supposed to be grateful or impressed that Terry knew everything about this place and was a poet.

They entered what looked like an office block but had a couple of small shops downstairs. Terry led Ralph to the elevator and they went to the top floor. When they emerged, they were in a cramped hallway. There were three grey doors, scratched and bruised, without handles and the place was silent. Ralph swallowed. There didn't seem to be a staircase. He was afraid and he didn't know why.

Terry swung one of the doors open and noise blared out. Ralph was relieved to see a bright and vibrant bar. He followed Terry inside. It seemed strange to have a bar so high up without windows. The room was spacious, though, with wooden tables, and an empty stage. Terry chose a table in the center with customers and waiters bustling past. Ralph would have picked a seat in the corner; now he felt exposed.

It was an ordinary bar, not a strip club, not anything Ralph had hoped for. Just a bar with people—mostly Japanese men in suits—drinking spirits and talking. Ralph had not remembered this friend-of-a-friend quite correctly. He'd imagined Terry leading a life in Tokyo as wild as his holiday in Thailand, but here he was talking about traditional musical instruments and being a poet. Ralph didn't want to admit now that he wasn't here on business at all, wasn't with any company. He would have liked to tell Terry about his shop in England but then it would be hard to explain why he was in Tokyo. Was it realistic that he would have come all the way to Japan to buy a few paints, some handmade paper? He couldn't tell Terry about the agency. He'd laugh.

Terry ordered drinks in Japanese. He seemed comfortable, chatting to the staff, flirting with the girl who cleared their table. Ralph tried not to be jealous. He would have his turn soon enough.

"So, are you interested in poetry?" Terry put his hand into his shirt pocket and produced a small notebook.

"I suppose I'm more of a visual arts person. Sketching. I don't know much about poetry—"

"Tell me what you think of this one." He looked at the paper, furrowed his brow, and pursed his lips before saying, "Sliced pink flesh glistens in dark seaweed envelopes, rotating sushi."

The words came out all pushed together. It took Ralph a moment to separate them and work out what he had heard. Terry looked eagerly for a response.

"Be honest."

"Is that the title? It's a bit long. I would just call it, 'Sushi,' not that I've eaten any myself since—"

"No, that's the poem. It's a haiku. It only has seventeen syllables you see. But it's supposed to have a word in it that indicates season and I couldn't see how to put one in. I don't think I've quite got it right yet. It probably doesn't matter. At this stage, it's the idea that's important."

"I see."

"But food is my theme at the moment. The thing is, I'm working on a collection of food haiku. I'm trying to do one about Big Macs to contrast with the sushi. I might bring the teriyaki burger into that one as a suggestion of East meeting West. That's got six syllables so I only need to add *a* or *the* and it would make up the middle line all by itself."

"It sounds interesting." Ralph stared into his drink. He had nothing to add to a conversation about counting syllables.

"I hope you don't mind my trying this out on you. My girlfriend speaks pretty good English but she doesn't get all the subtleties of poetry. If I read any to her, she just says out of politeness that she likes it. When I talk about getting my haiku published, she says she doesn't think they're quite *Japanese*, but of course they're not supposed to be. I'm writing in English."

"Is she oriental?" Ralph got a hard-on at the thought of Terry's girlfriend. He wanted to hear Terry talk about the relationship so that he could imagine it.

"Pardon? Oh, my girlfriend. Well, yes. She's Japanese."

"How did you meet her?"

"I used to teach an English literature class in the evening, part time. She was one of my students."

"Really? I bet you taught her a thing or two. So was it easy, I mean, getting a date with her?"

"I suppose so. It was just two people getting together, you know." Terry shrugged.

Ralph didn't know. He fiddled with the end of his new tie. He heard his stepfather's voice, *if you want to know then you'd better bloody ask*.

"Did you know from the beginning, then? I mean, that she was right for you. Could you tell that she liked you?"

"We hit it off in class." Terry smiled. It was almost a smirk. "I thought she was cute so I asked her out."

"Did you? You just asked her out after class? Lucky bastard, being a teacher here. You must be fighting them off every day. What's she like?"

Terry looked blank. "Hard to put a whole person into a few words. One day I'll write a haiku about her and send it to you." He frowned again, as he had before reciting his haiku. "I will crystallize her into seventeen syllables and her season will be spring because she was born in March. Yes, that's good." He paused for a moment as if trying to start composing it now, then thought better of it. "So what did you say your business was?"

"It's a small business. Does your girlfriend work?"

"Yes. She works for a travel agency. She's been there a few years."

"How nice. Does she . . . ? Is it . . . ?" but he couldn't think of another question. He wanted to know how they looked together, what they talked about, how often they had sex, and what she was like in bed. But what could he ask that would elicit such confidences?

Terry was beginning to look at Ralph closely and Ralph wondered if he had asked too much already. The lights in the bar dimmed and there was gentle applause. The stage lit up. Terry glanced around.

"There are dancers tonight. I'd forgotten which day it was. Looks like you're in luck."

Ralph's spirits rose. This was more like it. Now he could relax and settle into the evening, knowing the whole day had not been wasted.

"Good. It'll be like being back in Bangkok."

Terry's mobile phone rang and he went into a corner to have a conversation with a finger in one ear. The phone was pale blue, glittery—a girl's phone—and tiny in Terry's bulky hand.

Ralph sipped scotch and shut his eyes to concentrate on the burn in his throat. He imagined the girl in the powder-blue uniform, dancing for him. She was so fresh and groomed. Was she capable even of taking off her uniform? She wouldn't be nearly as sweet in a pair of jeans and a T-shirt. But what would her underwear be? He imagined some bright butterfly color, soft and clean, just covering enough of her flesh for him to want to push his fingers under the lacy edges and peel it all away. When he opened his eyes, four dancers had appeared in a far corner, pulling at sequined dresses. The music from the speakers changed and they began to dance, wiggling their hips a lot but with no rhythm. Every now and again they noticed the customers and remembered to smile but if you looked at their faces and ignored their bodies, you would think they were standing in a line for the bus.

They made Ralph uncomfortable. Each of the four faces reminded him not of the girl in the elevator, but of Apple. Their cool unsurprised eyes, arched brows, and soft noses all belonged to Apple. Was she intent on haunting him just as he was over his loss and about to find happiness again? But he looked for differences and there were plenty. Apple could move well, never looked vacant. She was thin but shapely, and her skin was soft and firm. These girls were not so clean-looking. They were scrawny. The lighting was wrong, he was tired, and their bodies were just writhing sacks of loose flesh. He drained his whisky glass. Terry was back.

"Japanese women are sweet." Ralph was thinking of the girl in the elevator.

"They're not Japanese. They're Filipinas, as far as I know."

Terry was so cool talking about the women. He thought he knew it all. Ralph felt small and unsuccessful, as if he had arrived too late. The Orient was meant to be his own discovery, his own piece of brilliance, but it turned out that people like Terry had got there first. He could hate Terry, or he could learn from him. And there were many things to learn.

"Another drink, Terry?"

"Why not? Are you on expenses?"

"Not exactly."

"Then don't pay. You have to be on a yen salary to get drinks here. You buy me a pint back in the Happy Man when I'm next over. I'll get these." He made no move to get the drinks. "So are you here for diplomacy or are they actually making you do stuff? Your company, I mean."

"Do stuff? Yes, meetings and things. Possible orders for products."

Terry's mobile rang again. He answered, saying *washing-machine*, then mumbled into the receiver. Ralph found it hard to believe that Terry could hear anything in the din of the music.

"Sorry Ralph. Gotta go. My girlfriend's come home from work early and doesn't understand why I'm not there. Give me a call if you want to go out again."

And Ralph was alone. No one to talk to for the rest of the evening. It was just bad luck, he knew that, but he wished he could join one of the other tables. He wouldn't want to talk, just sit among them with his glass in one hand and not look so solitary.

One of the women was dancing at him. She wiggled and gyrated like a whore. But Ralph was not turned on anymore. He was still thinking of Apple. Perhaps she really was innocent when he met her, just spoiled. He had been innocent, too. He didn't know what to do when faced with silence and stillness, couldn't see how to make anything of Apple. It would not happen again, not like that, because he wouldn't choose wrongly again.

A waiter appeared. Ralph caught his eye.

"One whisky," he said slowly and clearly, holding up his right index finger to make sure the waiter understood.

"One whisky. Yes. Just a moment, please." The waiter smiled nervously, as if this language were a distant memory from school days not the International Language, and slunk away to the bar.

Ralph watched people come and go through the main door, more men chattering loudly, probably straight from work. It was better than looking at the dancers. He gulped his whisky.

Terry hadn't left any cash so Ralph paid for the drinks with money that was supposed to last a week. He found his way back to the station by following the crowds on the pavements. They stretched all the way in a fat snake. His head twisted this way and that to see the faces that passed in the opposite direction. It was a strain having to take so many people into his vision at once. Some of the girls had frightening faces—dark make-up with bleached hair (didn't they know their black hair was one of their assets?) and too much shiny, pale lipstick—so then he tried to keep his eyes on people's backs. Apparently the buildings in this district were very high and impressive but he wasn't planning to look up and find out.

A woman asked him in English if he was lost and would like help. He was sure that he had seen her before. Was she one of the dancers? But she was Japanese. He wanted to say yes, but she had already gone. He looked around at all the women in their bright clothes and high heels. All were strangers. He bought a medium-priced ticket and waited at the end of the platform where the crowds were smaller.

In the carriage he had another experience with a woman.

The day had been rich in female contact. There was a young girl sitting next to him and she fell asleep, rested her head on his shoulder. Was she coming on to him? Or was she just an innocent child trusting the nearest adult for support? He watched her reflection in the window opposite. She was perhaps still in her teens. Her hair was bleached at the ends, unkempt. Her boots came up to her knees, had thick yellowish soles like pieces of cheese. Her skirt was a short, frilly rag-dollish thing. If he could just touch the hem, rub it between his finger and thumb, slip his hand beneath it onto her naked thigh.

The railway line curved and Ralph took the opportunity to lean into the girl. Their arms touched, pressed together and the girl sat up straight with a start. Wide-eyed she stared at her reflection, unblinking. She remained rigid in that position until the train stopped again. Then she stood and left, walking with a slight stoop as the high boots pushed her spine forward. How could her mother let her wear such heels?

Back at the hotel he broke open a packet of nuts from the minibar. As he nibbled them, one by one, he decided that he would marry a C-lister. He would find a pleasant charming woman, a little past her prime if necessary, and then go home. It was too hectic and confusing being alone in such a city. He bit on something that tasted funny. He stuck out his tongue and, from among the crunched-up peanuts, pulled off a tiny silver dead fish. He tossed it on the floor. He would claim his reward and leave this country at the first possible opportunity.

Five

Runa ran, half limping, through the trees. She pushed away tall weeds with her arms, found a gap in the fence. She reached the road and paused for breath. Nearby, a woman was digging around the bases of the bamboo trees for shoots. Her figure was small in the woods, scrabbling at the earth like a thief hunting for buried treasure. Runa kept her head down and sneaked past. The old woman paid no attention. Perhaps it was the one who had called out that night when Runa was on the roof with Jun. The hills in the distance were dark, barely visible. The village was asleep. Runa looked closely at each house and shop as she passed, knowing she would not see them again.

A bicycle glinted against the wall of the convenience store, a nice new blue one with a sharp black shopping basket. She scribbled a note thanking the owner for its use and stating where it could be collected the next day. As an afterthought she took a thousand-yen note—more than enough for a bus ticket to the station—and pushed it under a stone with the message. That was what Nanao would do. It was time Runa started trying to be a good and responsible person, like Nanao. She climbed onto the bicycle and swooped down the hilly road that led from the village, lifting her feet off the pedals and sticking her legs out.

Soon she was out in the countryside, cycling between rice paddies, following the narrow section of path that was lit by the bike's lamp. Frogs croaked in the marshes and Runa croaked back, laughing at the sound of her voice. She took a short cut through the fields to the river. The riverside path was straight and led directly to the next village. There were a few single lights dotted along the other side of the river. Runa supposed they must belong to fishermen but there was no sound, no sign of people. Her eyes were growing accustomed to the blackness and now she could see the mountains more clearly. She cycled faster. She had never liked to be alone in the dark. That was probably why she had fallen for Jun Ikeda, for company in the dark. Already the memory of Jun was making her cry. But even as the tears slipped across her face, she knew that crying was narcissistic. As much as she thought of Jun, she was also picturing her own pretty face, the tears, the romance lost, the tragedy of running away. She couldn't help seeing herself through Jun's eyes, beautiful even when she was disastrous.

The path grew quieter. Runa listened to the bicycle's wheels, humming like a single mosquito in the night. But after a few minutes it started to sound as if there were two bicycles, as if the other one was close behind her. It was hard to imagine who else might be traveling out here by the river so late at night, unless she was being followed. She pedaled faster but the noise stayed right behind her, just a meter or two away. She braked abruptly and stopped with one leg on the path. There was no noise, just the quiet pushing of the river and her own breath. She was imagining too many things.

She set off again and headed for the town. She could see the shapes of buildings, distant street lights, the fences and footbridges of the station. She would cycle to the next town, or the one after that, however many it took until she was on time for the first train of the morning. It was just too bad about the borrowed bicycle.

She made a detour because there was someone she wanted to see before she disappeared, just in case she was not imagining things and wasn't alone. In the suburbs, nestled among the houses, was a row of buildings. A couple of shops, a bar, and the Octopus karaoke place. She leaned the bicycle against the wall of the bar. It was a large brick cube with few windows. From the outside it was nothing special. Inside there were six or seven tables, a long bar with several stools. This was where she had first met Jun. No, not the very first time she met him; that was in the classroom. But it was when she first sighted him outside school, in his own clothes, and she forgot that he was a pupil. She knew his face, his name, but as if he were a friend she didn't see often, she was pleased to see him, couldn't place him. No one would ever believe her—out here in the middle of nowhere, it was hard to know people who weren't from the school—but seeing him in his jeans, he looked like a young man in his early twenties. And she was a young woman in her mid-twenties. Of course, she realized within two minutes that he was Jun Ikeda from the fifth year. But in those two minutes she had seen him as an adult.

He shouldn't have been there. Perhaps that confused her too. It was brave of an under-age teenager to venture into a bar, especially one within a couple of kilometers of the school. Teachers rarely came here—they went to more sophisticated places in the city—so he may have thought he was safe. Runa had come because she'd had a particularly tiresome day at school and needed fast escape and peace. Usually she went farther afield. Some of the others thought it strange that she, a woman, would drink alone in a bar but Runa liked a beer or a whisky once in a while, so that was what she did. Sometimes she went out with the other female teachers but they worked so much harder than she did in the evenings, planning their lessons and writing tests. If no one was free to go with her, she went by herself but quietly, not telling anyone.

He was with a couple of older boys—a brother, perhaps, and a friend—and they appeared to be leaving together as Runa entered. Runa did not notice his face then. She only paid attention when she saw that one of the boys had come back indoors and was ordering a drink at the bar. Then he sat beside her, glanced quickly at her face a few times with warm eyes, and said hello. Runa looked back and smiled because she knew him. Then the two minutes passed and she realized how she knew him. She gulped her drink. The situation was strange but she wanted to laugh. There was something about the promise of trouble that made her want to lick her lips, rub her hands together. Or perhaps that's just how she remembered it, knowing the excitement that followed.

Of course, she knew that they must leave the bar. He had ordered a drink and she, a high-school teacher, had witnessed this. If it were discovered, she would be in trouble and that would not be funny. And here she was with a good-looking man who was certainly attracted to her and appeared to be flirting, in a fashion.

His hands were beautiful. Soft, brown, straight fingers, one hand resting on the bar, the other on his knee, relaxed but still. Clean pink fingernails with perfect half-moons. Not a trace of nerves. Not a hint from anything he did that he was only sixteen.

She sensed adventure. His smile was faint and shy but his eyes were searching. She was captivated.

"We must leave," she said, "or this will be no good for either of us."

"Now?"

"In a minute, then. I don't want to go without finishing my drink."

"You live in the teachers' apartments next to the school grounds. I've seen you on your way home."

"Have you?"

"I live near. You go out a lot in the evenings. I've seen you."

"You've been watching me?"

"Is it because you hate living so close to the school that you are always going out? I would do the same."

"No. I don't hate it at all. But I like to go out even if I'm not really going anywhere. I've never been very good at staying indoors. It's just the way I am."

"You go to school until you're eighteen, then you go to university—which is the same thing—and then you end up back in a school for the rest of your life. In the middle of the countryside with nothing else around. And you go and live right next to the school. No escape. I can't understand being a teacher. If I were you I wouldn't want to live round here. Do you notice the boys in class?"

"I notice everyone. It's my job."

"You're laughing at me. What I mean is, how do you look at the boys? Do you think we're all just kids?"

"I don't think about it."

"What about me? Do you think of anything when you look at me at school?"

"No. I don't know. You're confusing me. Maybe I do, but I'm not aware of it. Did you follow me here tonight?"

"No. I came with my friends. I was excited when you appeared. Don't worry about them. They're not from school and they don't know who you are. Can we go out together one day? Away from this place, where no one will know us?"

"We can't do that. Besides, you'd have to have a car and go all the way to the mountains to be safely far enough."

"Have you been drinking with any of the boys before?"

"No. You're the only one."

"Don't you have boyfriends? You're pretty."

"I don't have a boyfriend at the moment."

"If you were my girlfriend, it would be even harder at school because we'd have to pretend there was nothing between us, but in another way it would be good because we'd have a secret and it would make school life more bearable. Why aren't you a model or an actress? Don't laugh."

"Sorry. I never thought about being an actress. I just sort of ended up being a teacher."

"I'll never understand. What a choice!"

"It wasn't exactly a choice. I needed a job. But I wouldn't want to be an actress or a model. If I could do anything, I'd have my own bar. I'd like to work in it all night, every night, and sleep during the day. People would be coming and going all the time and I would talk to them all. I wouldn't be alone for a second."

"In the city?"

"It would be in the countryside with mountains all around, but not here, not anywhere near the school."

"I'd like to go there. I'd be your best customer. And when you needed anything done, I'd help you out, if you'd let me."

"Jun, you shouldn't be in a bar. You should leave. It's wrong for you to be here, and wrong for me to talk to you like this."

"I know. I know, but it's a strange place. There's no such thing as right or wrong behavior when you're out here in the hills. Did you know that Mr. Onda was seeing one of the girls in my class last term?"

"I heard a rumor. To be honest—"

"Teacher, what's your name?"

"My name? Wada. You should know—"

"I do know. Your first name."

"Runa. My name is Runa."

"That's a pretty name. Like lunar."

"That was why my father chose it. He was an avid astronomer. Actually, he wanted to call me *Moon*, in English."

"That would be funny. Why didn't he?"

"Too weird. And also, it sounded Korean. My mother said I'd get bullied at school. So they settled on Runa. That's the story my sister told me. I can't ask him now."

"Is he dead?"

"No. He went senile when my mother died."

"Sorry."

"Oh, it's all right. Everyone in my family goes senile, sooner or later. That's just how it is. He doesn't know where he is anymore but he's just as nice as ever, so I suppose that he must be quite happy."

"Your drink?"

"Almost finished."

"Then let's go."

Runa looked at the boy and saw how he had already turned the school—her whole life, those days—into nothing, just by being with her. The most ordinary facts of her life were exciting and dangerous because she was relating them to a schoolboy, and in a bar. She was filled with something warm, as if she wanted to burst into tears, but it wasn't quite that. She wanted to run around, faster than she knew she could, jump into boiling or freezing water. She put her glass into Jun's hand, let him sip her whisky. She was pushing herself to go too far, so that it would be too late to stop.

He was not bowing, not stammering or using honorific language when he addressed her. He was showing none of the respect he should, and she liked it. It was so natural; she saw no hint that he was acting. It was the other boy she knew, the one in the navy uniform behind the rickety wooden desk, who was the pretender. Jun handed her the glass with a drop of whisky left. She dipped her finger in, licked it.

She should never have said anything. She should have pretended not to see him and left quickly, but he was watching her, his lips parted, waiting for her to say what would happen next.

Jun Ikeda went home by bus and Runa by taxi. They arrived near the school at the same time though. No one was there to see them. Jun lifted Runa over the gate to the teachers' apartments that was shut every night at midnight. The black metal was slightly damp from rain that she hadn't realized had fallen. As her feet touched the concrete on the other side, she felt the thread of a spider's web across her face.

They didn't kiss. She didn't want to kiss him. It was enough that they had been together. In fact, she found Kawasaki that night and slept with him instead. She crept into his apartment when she knew he would be in a deep sleep and curled up next to him in his bed. In the morning she woke early and disappeared.

She thought that it had ended and did not feel any urge to kiss Jun Ikeda until the following afternoon when she saw him at school. He was there in the corridor, in his uniform, school bag over his arm, laughing happily with friends about something stupid a teacher had said. His white teeth flashed, unintentionally, in her direction. She walked right past and didn't look back. For the rest of the day she thought of nothing but Jun, and in her bed she missed him as if they'd been sleeping together for months.

A day or two later Jun came to see Runa with a question about English grammar. He had written out some English sentences and wanted to know if they were correct. Underneath he had written, in English, *Tonight in Octopus?* She took a red pen and wrote on it. "*The* Octopus," she said, as she rested her pen on the desk. "Don't forget the definite article. But apart from that, the answer is yes, it's fine."

Runa stood in front of it now. The Octopus karaoke place was a strange, angular building. Runa had never understood why it was called the Octopus. There was no picture of one above the door, no hint of anything octopus-like in the decor. The building's exterior was a mix of drab and gaudy. The walls were grey and the door was shabby and brown. A string of pink lights flashed around the door frame. Some bulbs were missing so the effect was of a gap-toothed smile. The windows were small and dirty. Runa looked and listened. It must be past closing time but the lights were on and a few people were moving around inside. Sometimes it seemed to stay open all night, serving drinks, letting people sing themselves hoarse. Out here the police didn't bother to check what was going on. But she'd heard that business was dwindling and it was to be shut down, replaced by a brand new *pachinko* parlor.

Runa was glad that it would soon cease to exist but wanted to find the owner. She had to talk to him. She pushed open the door and looked around. There was no one behind the desk so she called, *excuse me*, and paced around noisily. She peered into the room where all of this began. It was the smallest of the rooms, big enough only for three or four people. Tonight it was empty.

The intercoms were often broken, so when you ordered

drinks you couldn't be sure anyone had heard you. Sometimes the drinks arrived and sometimes they didn't. The carpets were old and smelled of cigarette smoke. Now that Runa thought about it, it was amazing that it had done so much business out in the countryside and with the neon sparkly Hollywood Dream only a few kilometers away. But the Octopus was special.

She and Jun had sung and danced in their tiny room for hours, then slept on the soft long seats. In the morning they found they were covered by blankets. The owner must have come in before locking up. He was known for looking after his customers. He never threw people out if there was no taxi for them, if they were too drunk to ride a bicycle. After that, though, Jun and Runa were more careful. It wasn't impossible that someone from the school would see them there. So they started to meet at weekends and headed straight for the mountains or the beach. They also began to visit love hotels.

She looked at the battered video screen in the corner of the room. She tried to remember the songs they sang. Silly pop songs mostly. It didn't matter. It struck Runa as funny that Jun sang a couple of English songs and with good pronunciation, as good as hers and she had studied English for years. In class he hadn't shown much ability at all.

She returned to the desk and waited.

She couldn't be sorry for what they had done. She would leave the school and would leave Jun Ikeda because she wouldn't be hunted and judged—and she hoped that nothing bad happened to Jun—but she couldn't imagine ever being sorry, no matter how hard she tried. They'd had fun. That was the point and she hoped that Jun, too, would never regret that he had met her.

She knocked on a door marked *private*. She must talk to the owner and ask if anyone had seen her with Jun. If so, who were they?

The door opened slowly. The owner, a grey-haired man in his sixties or seventies, peered through the gap.

"Hello. Did you want to book a room?" He looked over her shoulder for Jun.

"I wanted to ask a question."

He looked at Runa with surprise. His eyes were narrow and puffy as if he had just woken up but he was fully dressed. "Yes, of course. The small room is free at the moment. Are you sure you don't want—"

"No, thank you. I have to get going soon. I'm sorry to bother you—"

"That's all right. I've had so few customers this week. I thought I'd go to bed early. It's a warm night, isn't it? Can you hear the frogs outside?"

"Yes." She'd forgotten them but again noticed the din. "I just wanted to ask—"

"They're so noisy. It sounds as if there are hundreds of them and they're all big but in fact, if you go and look for them, there are only a few and they're tiny. You wouldn't think they could make such a noise."

"You remember when I used to come here, with a boyfriend?"

"Oh, yes."

"Do you think anyone was ever watching us, I mean, secretly? Did you notice anything?"

"No, I don't think so. I only ever saw the two of you, and I can tell you, I would have noticed if anyone were watching."

"I thought perhaps someone might have been interested, might have been hanging around to see what we were doing."

"I see. It's not impossible, but it's very quiet these days and I think you would have noticed, even if I hadn't."

"You're right. Thank you."

"That's all right. Well, I've got some cleaning to do." He headed back to the door.

"There's another thing. I'm leaving tonight. If my boyfriend comes here again, will you tell him I said goodbye?"

"Of course. Goodnight, then."

Outside, she climbed back onto the bike and bumped over uneven paving stones. She headed for the street lamps of the main road. It was a clear run now to the next town. She pedaled along humming in the warm night, humming the school song because it was the first that came to mind, though she had never learned all the words. In school assemblies she had always made sure she was behind all the other teachers so that she wouldn't have to sing, could get the giggles if the principal said something silly, and it wouldn't matter. Trees lined up along the roadside and the moon shone a path on the tarmac. She was running away, and it was not as bad as she'd thought it would be.

Six

It was a peculiar day. The sky was colorless and the temperature hard to guess—it seemed that it might be cooler than recent days, yet the air was close around Ralph—as if there was just no weather at all. He smoothed his hair and stepped into the agency.

There was no sign of Mr. K. A younger chap buzzed around in the office, handsome and tanned. He was joking with the receptionist, a chubby girl who laughed loudly at everything he said. Her face was familiar from the previous day, though she seemed to have taken on a new personality. He didn't recall hearing laughter before. Ralph was disoriented, wondered if he had come out onto the right floor.

"Excuse me, I have an appointment with the man I spoke to yesterday?"

"Hi. You must be Mr. Turnpike. Nice to meet you."

The young man spoke English with an American accent that was almost perfect. There was just something unclear about the ends of his words that gave him away as a foreigner. He shook Ralph's hand. Ralph felt the damp puffiness of his own fingers. His skin was a funny mottled mauve against the man's even brownness.

"My dad had to go to the dentist. His crown came out while he was eating a rice cracker. Would you believe it? They're always saying that the younger generation have weak teeth because they don't eat enough hard food, but I'm not so sure now. Usually he'd come to work even with a missing crown, but it was a front tooth so he was kind of self-conscious. Not good for the agency's image, I guess. So I'm looking after the place today. You'll have to excuse me. I've never done this before so I'm still learning the ropes myself."

And he said something in Japanese to the girl who was typing lists of names into a computer. She laughed without looking up. Her manicured fingers tapped away at the keyboard. Ralph wondered if she was typing the C list. He tried a smile. It almost hurt. He did not think he liked Mr. K.'s son.

"I'm supposed to be meeting two ladies. I have an appointment."

"Sure. Take a seat in the interview room. The first one'll be here any second."

Ralph entered the interview room and remembered with sadness and humiliation the A-list women he'd met there. At the time he had believed that he just had to choose and one would become his wife, like a prince and princess in a silly fairy tale.

The interview room was small but some attempt had been made to give the illusion of space. There were large unmatching framed mirrors on three of the white walls. Ralph's reflection appeared in two of them. But the mirrors were dirty and had greasy fingerprints around the edges. Last time the room had struck him as being light and clean but now he noticed the chipped paint around the door, the scratches on the tiled floor. There were two flowery armchairs, a low glass table holding up a delicate flower arrangement. And there were more potted plants, dusty and rubbery in each corner and flanking every piece of furniture. If the point was to create an atmosphere of warmth, somehow it didn't work. Each plant, each object in the room, seemed to have parachuted separately into the space and stood isolated from the others.

Ralph settled in the nearer armchair. He noticed a black plastic chair in the corner and hoped that the cocky young man would not be joining them. Then the interpreter, a young woman in tight trousers and a T-shirt, scurried through the door and Ralph realized that the chair was for her. C-list women wouldn't be able to speak English. She introduced herself briskly and sat down.

The first lady entered. She was aged about forty. She was a little overweight but had nice wavy hair and was quite attractive, until she smiled. Her teeth were grey, almost black, and jutted out from her gums at all angles. Ralph wondered how much it would cost him to have them put right; he could not get used to such a smile. He had read that cosmetic dentistry was becoming more affordable—though her teeth would need to be ripped out completely and started again—but it was probably beyond his reach. It would mean cashing in some savings that he had put by for a new roof. Still, he wouldn't want to be standing next to teeth like that in the pub. He wanted his neighbors to see his pretty wife, with her milk-teeth smile, not a wife who could be laughed at. He would not be laughed at. He focused on her eyes. They were shiny, uncertain, and he felt a pang of guilt. His own teeth were not perfect, not bad, but not perfect. He was here for love, after all, and she deserved a chance.

They shook hands. Her fingers were soft and waxy, little birthday-cake candles, and Ralph held on just a little bit longer than he would in a normal handshake. He wondered if this was the hand that would be in his all the way back to England, that he would slip a ring onto. She sat on the edge of her chair, wriggled her way back until she was comfortable, gave a nervous giggle. Her skirt stopped just above her knees and he noticed how thick, straight and smooth her legs were, like banister posts.

Ralph leaned back in his chair and put his questions as though interviewing her for a job. He would be courteous but was not going to bow and scrape to a C-lister.

"My name is Ralph. What is your name?"

She said something with three syllables that he couldn't catch. It didn't matter. He would hear it again later.

"Do you have a job?"

The interpreter told him that she worked in an office.

"Well," he said with a smile, "you won't have to do that if you come to England with me. I have a shop. And I have a house with four bedrooms and a big garden. Money is no problem."

He remembered that you were not supposed to brag in

Japan. If you talked about something that belonged to you, you had to be humble and say that it wasn't very good. You had to apologize for it, even if you were talking about a member of your own family. He couldn't work out how to do that and still convey the message that he would give her everything.

"I'm not a *very* rich man. My house is modest. But I have a steady income. And it's not a bad income. Not millions, of course, but . . ." His voice faded.

The interpreter told her. She nodded, still smiling, but that was her only reaction. Ralph wondered if she had understood correctly. He didn't trust the interpreter with her short hair, big pink earrings, and quick voice. He spoke to the lady directly.

"In England—my country—I have beautiful old house. Four bedrooms. And garden. Very good house."

The woman began to look nervous, though she was still smiling. Ralph wondered if she had understood a word.

"Do you have any hobbies?"

"I like swimming." So she could understand him.

"Nice. But can you draw? Picture?" He mimed. They would do better to avoid using the interpreter, if they could.

"I'm . . . I am not good at drawing."

"But you play the piano? Or the violin?" He paused for just a split second between the words.

She shook her head. "No, I can't."

He had thought that all Japanese women played instruments. "Didn't your family have money to pay for lessons?"

She looked nonplussed. The interpreter, hawkeyed,

glanced quickly between the two. He would ask more about her family.

"Do you live with your family now?"

"Yes."

"Are you very close to them?"

She shrugged. "Yes." Her voice was defensive, as if she wasn't sure why he was asking. She should see, though, why this was important to him.

"Because if you come to England with me, they would miss you very much."

"Yes. Maybe." She touched the tip of her nose, a sure sign of lying he had read, though he wasn't sure why she might be lying.

He was not getting to know her at all so he tried a more important topic.

"I was married before. This would be my second marriage. What is your relationship history?" He was talking louder now. He knew she wouldn't necessarily understand him better if he shouted but at least it wouldn't be his fault if she didn't.

She turned to the interpreter for help. The two women exchanged a few sentences—more than could possibly be necessary for such a simple question—and Ralph tapped his foot. The interpreter told him that the woman had never been married before.

"Boyfriends?"

The lady understood the question this time and shrugged with a smile. What was that supposed to mean?

Japanese girls are protected by their families but sex before marriage is very common in Japan, particularly when compared with

many other Asian countries. Try to see this in a positive light. As
soon as she is married your Eastern Blossom will be devoted to
you. Her experience will only enhance yours!

"Are you a virgin?"

"She doesn't want to answer that." The interpreter folded
her arms, fixed her gaze on Ralph.

"You haven't asked her."

"It's not a polite question. Do you think it's a polite question?"

"If she wants to marry me, she'll have to tell me a few
facts."

"I don't think so."

"I don't care what you think. I'm not asking you."

"It's not a polite question."

Ralph uncrossed his legs, let them swing apart and leaned
back.

"I assume, then, that she is not a virgin. Since she doesn't
wish to answer the question." Ralph was pleased with the
commanding tone of his voice.

"Come on. She's forty-seven. Do you expect her to be a
virgin?"

The interviewee was watching with an expression of
amazement. Ralph wondered how much of the discussion she
understood. If this strident young interpreter weren't here
poking her nose in, the whole business would be so much
nicer. But, still, *forty-seven*. She was old enough to be his . . .
well, she was too old to be his wife.

"Madam, you're here to interpret. I'm not here to solicit

your opinions so do not feel free to share them. Please do the job for which you are paid."

The interpreter ignored him, muttered something to the woman. The woman stood and waved her hand in front of her face as if there was a bad smell in the room. Ralph understood that this was a rejection.

"I'm sorry," she said. "No, thank you." And she left the room. The interpreter followed with her lips pressed smugly together. They were like two girlfriends in a pub, going off to the ladies' to moan about an unsatisfactory boyfriend. Before the door closed Ralph thought he caught the interpreter sticking her tongue out at him, but when he blinked she had gone and the door was shut.

The leaves of the plants trembled. Ralph had blown another chance. He thought over his questions. He had asked about her life, her family. What was wrong with that? He had told her that he had been married before. You couldn't start a relationship without knowing a few things. He didn't want to find his new wife was a slut. It was reasonable to ask; the agency wouldn't. He was honest and she must be, too. Besides, she was far too old. He was no closer to finding his wife. These women were all wrong. And yet, he had seen her, the perfect one. She was in the department store. And in so many forms on the streets. He smoothed his hair and watched as the doorknob turned and the door creaked back open.

The second lady was younger—perhaps thirty-five or forty—and Ralph felt a prickle of hope. She had a soft face, reminded him of a kind primary school teacher. A wide smile and glinting eyes. She wasn't exactly pretty—her chin was too big—but you could look at her without feeling bad. He wouldn't mind being seen in public with her. She introduced herself in good English as Aki. He liked her simple name.

She told Ralph how she had always wanted to get away from Japan and go abroad. She wanted to pursue her career as an engineer and said that it was hard for a woman to be a successful engineer in Japan. She explained about the working hours in Japan, the lack of holidays, the effect of the recession on promotion. When she paused long enough for Ralph to speak, he could think of nothing to say. It didn't matter. She continued regardless, a steamroller on a thin country lane.

"So I'd like to do a masters at a British university and then find work there. Of course, I need to do some work on my English first."

Was she a gold-digger? She might expect him to pay for her university education and then be out all day and night, furthering her career. If Ralph had wanted to pay thousands of pounds for a masters course, he would have done one himself. It was ridiculous. He would not be an open wallet to fund her self-centered ambitions. He looked at her closely, narrowed his eyes.

"What do you want me for?"

She looked surprised. "Pardon?"

"Why do you want a British husband?"

"I want to get married. If I stay here and marry a Japanese man, it'll be the end of my career, I'm sure. You just can't work the hours here and have a family. But I don't want to be single forever. I want to grow old with someone. Why does anyone want to get married?"

"For love."

"Love? Yes, OK. That's part of it." She nodded slowly as if still thinking about her answer.

"Love is all of it." He said this irritably. His nose was itchy, probably from all these plants. He would have loved to take out his hankie and blow his nose hard, but apparently that was bad manners in Japan. Instead, he sniffed, repeatedly.

Aki was not the kind of woman he wanted to meet. She was the kind of woman he had hoped to get away from. She completely misunderstood the point of men and women marrying, and was obsessed with her own career. She hadn't asked Ralph a single question about himself.

"Is there anything you'd like to know about me?"

Aki reached into her bag, pulled out a lighter and packet of cigarettes. She lit up nonchalantly, as if not aware she was doing it, and puffed smoke into Ralph's face.

"How old are you?" She raised her eyebrows.

"Would you put that cigarette out, please?" He coughed loudly to make it clear.

She seemed surprised and looked at the glowing end of the stick as if someone had just put it into her hand.

"Sorry. I find myself smoking when I'm nervous. Shall I open a window?"

"I'm on medication. It's bad for me." Ralph became more stressed at the sound of his own raised voice. "Put out that cigarette now."

Aki stood, ground her cigarette into her empty and left it there.

"I want to meet a gentleman. I don't like you," she said and clattered out of the room. Ralph expected the door to slam behind her but it didn't. It creaked slowly and shut with a barely audible click.

He cupped his hands over his mouth to breathe without inhaling smoke. He felt shaky. He was going to stop breathing. He was going to die. Why would no one help him?

The young man popped his head around the door. Ralph was rigid with hate and wanted to punch him. The man smiled broadly as if Ralph were his favorite uncle.

"No luck then? I'm sorry about that. Maybe you'd like to come by again some time. Potato chip?" He held out a large bag. "Sweetcorn and seaweed flavor. Bet you don't get those in England. They're good." He put three or four chips into his mouth at once and crunched.

Ralph stood, shaking, and jabbed the air in front of Mr. K.'s son with his finger.

"I'm not hungry. I've wasted enough time here, thank you. I saved up for this trip for months and all I asked was that you live up to your promise of helping me find a suitable wife. I can't hang around forever you know, coming and going without any help from you. I have a life to get on with. This has been a disaster from start to finish and none of it is my fault. I've had a wife before. You're insulting me. I'm not C-list and I won't—"

"Perhaps it's just not for you. Maybe you're not the marrying type. Hey, I know for sure I'm not."

Ralph pushed the plastic chair out of his way and clattered into the reception area. Mr. K.'s son followed. The secretary was nibbling chips delicately from a piece of paper that had been folded carefully to make a little chip-holding boat. When she saw him she wiped her fingers on a handkerchief and put the boat under her desk. She busied herself at her computer, as if trying to appear professional.

Ralph turned to Mr. K.'s son and eyed the bag of chips. He was hungry and would have loved to grab a handful but he must remain aloof and indignant.

"I was married to a Thai lady and met lots of other nice ladies in Thailand who wanted to marry me. The agencies there were better. They provided me with so many possibilities, I couldn't even meet them all." His voice cracked on every fourth or fifth word and he sounded to himself like a boy on the edge of puberty. "I had the pick of Thailand. You may not see what I have to offer but plenty of other people certainly do."

"I can't say I know much about agencies in other countries. You could go back there—"

"No, I can't. And I don't have to tell you why."

"You don't." The young man dropped his voice, spoke calmly. "You don't have to tell me anything at all, Mr. Turnpike. I can't argue with you there."

"You promised to find me a suitable match."

"Sorry. As I mentioned before, I don't usually work here. Personally, I didn't promise you anything. Sometimes I guess there's no such thing as a suitable match. There's only so much you can do. If you don't mind my saying so, you're kind of getting a bit old, aren't you? I'm not an expert here, but I'd say that's your problem. This is Japan." He stroked his thick shiny hair as he spoke. "See, these women are looking for glamour or a life abroad or something—I don't know what—but they're not actually desperate. I mean it's not like they're starving and have to get out of the country to send money back to their families. You might do better in a Third World country."

Mr. K.'s son took a step forward, forcing Ralph to move closer toward the door. Ralph realized that he was being edged out of the office. He squared his shoulders and stood firm.

"That shouldn't be an issue. These women—they don't show respect. Your advertisement is lying. I've come all the way from England. I should have been told before I left that they were going to be opinionated and rude. You should put that in your brochure. 'Opinionated and Rude Ladies Who Aren't Interested in Marrying You.' How else can I know, if you don't tell me? I've spent a lot of money. I'm not a rich man, you know. I'm not made of money. I don't think much of this set up at all. That woman smoked without even asking me first. Do you call that manners?"

The man cocked his head to one side as if considering. He smiled broadly.

"She's cute though, ha? Face isn't perfect, but nice ass. Wonder why she's on the C list. I could see her as a kind of Japanese Meg Ryan. Sorry. What did you say? She smoked? I do apologize. She shouldn't have done that. This whole office is supposed to be no-smoking but it's hard to stop people when they're nervous. It's give and take with our clients, you know. Like marriage. Ha ha."

Ralph wanted to go home, wanted to be in his shed away from people, wanted a cup of tea, or a pint with Barry. He was making a spectacular fool of himself, but he would never be here again. He would say his piece and not hate himself later for being scared.

"That's of no interest to me. Being as nice about her as I can, I'd say she was too Westernized."

"You call it Westernization, Mr. Turnpike," the young man said with his charming smile and a swish of long eyelashes, "I call it progress. Goodbye. Have a safe journey home. Hope you meet the woman of your dreams."

He opened the door wide to show Ralph out.

"Oh, I will. The problem here isn't me. No. Because I'm looking for love. True love. And I'll find it."

"I do hope so. I'll ask my dad about getting you a refund but I've a feeling he'll say no."

And he closed the door, leaving Ralph in the thick heat.

Ralph blinked furiously as he looked along the street for a taxi. This was not his fault. It was not possible that he could be wrong. No, he was not wrong and he would not lose hope.

Seven

Not feeling that she had been either awake or asleep, Runa lay still, thinking about where she was, the place she had landed. It was too much trouble to open her eyes but she thought she was awake. And she didn't know where she was. Not the school—she remembered leaving. And she wasn't in China yet. She thought she could recall the shape of the room, and with her eyes closed could map the space. There was a wall immediately to her left that had a window. Or a wardrobe. Yes, perhaps it was a wardrobe and not a window. There was certainly something halfway along that wall. And, opposite, a door. She was in a hotel room. In Kobe. She'd needed a hotel for the night. It was coming back.

She had arrived in the city (on a bicycle? Could that be right?) and looked around to find a place to sleep. Then she was walking. Business hotels, capsule hotels, a towering glass-and-brick hotel with fountains and shiny bellboys swinging in and out. She liked the bellboys—so sweet, they caught her eye—but she needed a hotel without staff to recognize her. Where would no one think to look for her, if they were looking? Where would there be no record or memory of her stay? She wandered through Chinatown, followed the breeze toward the port, found what she was looking for. A love hotel. She checked in, spoke to no one.

The room was all purple. The carpet was soft, the curtains velvety. There was a large heart-shaped bath at the other end of the room, purple and pink stripes. The television looked new and expensive. Beside it was a list of films. From her position on the bed Runa couldn't read the words but saw little pictures of women in black underwear, in school uniforms, in nurse's outfits. They were all smiling at Runa, which seemed odd. And what about after sex? Didn't people ever just want to watch cartoons afterward? At the other love hotels, the ones she had been to with Jun Ikeda, she ignored the pornography. She didn't care about the shape of the baths. The hotels were just places where they could be alone, that guaranteed secrecy, at least for an hour or two. They were never luxurious. This one was better equipped and cleaner. The carpet didn't smell of cigarette smoke. It was altogether a better class of love hotel. Yet she was alone, and for a whole night.

She wondered if Nanao had ever stayed in a love hotel. Her first thought was that she hadn't but now that she gave it some consideration, she imagined that Nanao might have. One of those boyfriends Nanao used to meet in the afternoons after lectures. Always kind and gentle men, all of them shy, none of them quite good-looking, always completely besotted with Nanao. Ken-something, Masa-something, Taka-something.

Runa recalled that they all wore glasses. She had liked each one of them but she couldn't remember now which was which. When Nanao was a student she had shared a room with another girl so a love hotel would have been useful. It showed that Runa didn't know her sister as well as she should. She said aloud, *What about me Nanao? Do you think that Jun Ikeda was the only one? Do you think that was just a terrible mistake, or do you know me better?*

Now that she was in a safe place, she must prepare her journey. She reached into her bag for her address book and found her friend's phone number on a piece of paper tucked inside. It was written in Ping's handwriting and Runa smiled at the memory of their last meeting. It would be so good to see her again, let Ping sort out the next stage of her life. Maybe Ping would be ready for adventure too and they could set off together. Ping was an expert at forged passports, new jobs. And if she was not at home, her family would be there. She had a large family, lots of aunts and uncles, cousins.

Runa dialed the number. It rang a couple of times and a man answered. She spoke in Japanese.

"Is Ping there?"

He was silent, then said something in Chinese. Runa tried English.

"May I speak to Ping please?"

"Ping?"

"My friend. Is she at home?"

There was a pause. "No. I don't know Ping. Not this number." He hung up.

Tears welled. Ping might be out, of course, but to Runa it

sounded as if the man had never heard of her. For the first time, she began to doubt her plan. If Ping wasn't there, if Runa couldn't find her, then there was nowhere to go. She didn't have another plan. She would have to go to China and look for her friend. Ping would have to be there.

Runa lay back on the love hotel bed, worn out again by the exertion of the telephone call. She reached for a light switch, pressed something beside the bed. The lighting didn't alter but she discovered that she was moving. The bed was revolving slowly. She didn't like it—it was so unnecessary and also made an annoying buzzing sound—but didn't try to stop it. Instead she shut her eyes and let herself go round and round.

Soon she was half dreaming, worrying about where she was going to finish up, and about invisible lovers in her room, warm in couples, all around her and above her bed. They woke her each time she felt herself slipping into sleep. They made her nervous, exposed. She wanted Jun Ikeda. She wanted someone, anyone, to soak up the space in the sheets.

And a little later her feet sank into the warm furry carpet. She walked toward the bath and wondered how she would sit in such an odd shape. She turned on the taps, then glanced at the video menu, because it was there. The programs did not look nice, were not to her taste, too many pictures of young girls, where were the men? She ran a bath and added a sachet of pink powder from a fur-covered basket. The room was having sex all around her, in the shadows of all the furtive people who had been there before. It was impossible not to think of them—the businessman and the schoolgirl, the married couple who lived in one room with their children, the two corporate colleagues who couldn't get privacy in the company housing—they were all here. She could almost smell them. The feeling they created together was not loving but cold and somehow brutal. When Runa went to a love hotel with Jun she forgot that anyone else ever used them. And now she saw the image of Jun Ikeda everywhere she looked, everywhere he should be—soaking in the bath, lying on the bed resting his head on one hand, in the doorway with his arms folded. She felt left out and left behind. Lonely.

When the bath was full, she sank down in the pink fizzing water, leaned back into the point of the heart, drew her knees to her chest, closed her eyes. She moved her hand up and down her legs and let them rest on her thighs. Then she slipped her fingers between her legs, inside herself, and lay in that position, breathing slowly. She could hear the people who had been in this room. Echoing swimming-pool voices around the bath that gasped, whispered, giggled, coughed, and cried. If you liked it, it could be a whole evening's entertainment. The bath water turned cold. She stood, and dripped a little blood. So she was not pregnant after all. Still, she wouldn't ever go back to Jun. It was enough to know that she could have been.

Wet and shivering, she returned to the purple bed, too stiff to dress. She must use the telephone, must speak to someone. She checked through all the information, wondering if there was a number she could use to call a man. Any man that she could borrow, to help her stop thinking of Jun. Or hire—Runa would pay. Just to keep her company for the night. She wouldn't ask for more. But there wasn't. Of course there wasn't. Where could she find one? Someone to sleep beside, just someone there to be warm against her skin. There were the bellboys she had seen, so polished up, on display and ready to be used. She could go and find them, find one. See if he wanted to earn some extra money. But even as she thought it, she knew she couldn't leave the bed. It was a thought that just went through her mind, but she wouldn't do it. *Well*, she thought, *perhaps I will find love in China. But first, I will need some new documents. I must find Ping.*

Eight

Ralph logged onto the hotel computer. There was a message from his half-brother about the weather. Storms in England. Ralph's garage door had come off and Barry was worried about the house, especially the roof. Should he get builders round to look at the roof just in case? Did Ralph know when he would be back?

When I'm ready, Barry, and not before. When I have found her.

If he couldn't have a Japanese one, he'd simply have to try another country. He couldn't go home unmarried or without, at the very least, a fiancée.

He scrolled through his inbox to find the message sent a couple of weeks before by a Chinese woman named Li Hua. He'd spotted her on the Internet and they wrote to each other a few times before Ralph thought of coming to Japan. She seemed friendly and pleasant so he had asked her for a photograph. It arrived about three weeks later and Ralph was afraid to open it. He did, after a couple of cans of beer, and his fears were confirmed. She had said she was thirty-two (which was already older than he wanted) but she looked about forty-five. Her face was round and ordinary, slightly mannish. He put the photo back into the envelope and didn't look at it again. He tried to imagine her into something better, something prettier. Something, he saw with hindsight, a bit like the elevator girl. And then he almost convinced himself that she would do.

But a week or so later he saw a man in the pub with a beautiful Asian woman at his side. The man introduced her to his friends as Yoko. Ralph, listening in from his stool at the bar, realized he hadn't once thought of Japan. He found the agency in Tokyo and forgot about Li Hua. Now he needed her. He couldn't afford to be away from home much longer and he didn't have time to start again from scratch. With Li Hua, half the work was already done.

> *Dear Miss Li Hua*
>
> *It was lovely to hear from you again! I would be extremely delighted to meet you very soon. I will arrive in Shanghai on Wednesday by ferry because the planes are all booked up. I can assure you I am serious and I won't waste your time. I am definitely thinking of love and marriage, not just something superficial, although I am very happy to go entirely at your pace. I hope you are looking forward to meeting me too.*
>
> *Yours sincerely*
> *Ralph Turnpike (BA)*

In his room he read again a bit of the Chinese section of *Eastern Blossoms*.

For the traditional Chinese woman, loyalty and devotion are central to her life. The most important thing for her is the family. Nowadays, many Chinese women work, but don't let this worry you! It is the same almost everywhere and anyway they will not try to outshine their husbands because they are loyal and respectful. She will support you and not question your decisions. You may show your respect for her in the home by allowing her to take charge of trivial matters such as keeping the cupboards stocked and ordering the milk. There is no need to over-assert yourself and we do not condone domestic violence. The Asian ladies like men who are firm while being polite and gentle.

She sounded lovely, whoever she was. Ralph took his pills, washing them down with beer from the minibar. He shouldn't, but once in a while it was good. It helped him imagine things, helped him relax so he could pretend things about his life. He shut his eyes and remembered the most beautiful and most destructive woman in his life.

Apple. Sitting in the bath, shiny white foam up to her neck and in meringue blobs on her sticking-out legs. He watches from the doorway. He has come in from the shop so his clothes smell of cardboard and money. He goes to the bedroom, changes into lighter, looser clothes. Then she is beside him on the silky carpet, slipping a blue dress over her head, brushing her hair. It rises with static then falls, spreading over her shoulders like black oil. By the front door she pulls on sandals, with the buckles already fastened. Her ankles wobble as she balances to pull the straps over her heels. He asks where she is going. She doesn't answer, closes the door softly as she leaves. He doesn't know how to stop her, what he will do next. He is shaking and his legs fill with a strange warmth, as if he is wetting himself. In the bathroom again, he is watching her in the bubbles.

And the scene repeated and repeated. He imagined the hotel bed was a magic carpet and he soared away from Japan, over all the countries in Asia—where he saw the most beautiful women in the world, ready to be plucked—and toward his very own house and garden in England. His castle and his kingdom.

Nine

Later Runa dressed, left the loveless hotel behind her, and caught a bus to the port. The sky was half light, half dark. It could be dawn or dusk. As the bus pulled into a stop at the port, it opened out into sunshine. Then she glimpsed the sea and smiled. She walked into the departure area at the port, swinging her bag in the sunny room. She was pleased to be there, but only because of the sunshine and the sea. She knew that if it were raining, she would not be feeling so light. This was not a holiday, after all. She found a wall made entirely of window and pressed her face against it. The sea was a strange shade of turquoise, as if dyed extra blue for the benefit of the travelers. Maybe, like the flawless round red apples in the supermarkets, they had now managed to color and perfect the sea.

Runa's stomach churned when she imagined sailing out on it, over it. The blue reached so far she could hardly believe it had another side, where it may, for all she knew, be raining. It seemed dangerous, perhaps impossible. But she had to go. She wanted to be at the other side without the journey in between. It would be better not to look, better not to think about the sea and how hard it was to believe in the blueness.

The last time she'd watched the sea she had been with Jun. Runa had rented a car and they'd driven away over the mountains to where they would never be found. Runa enjoyed winding through the steep roads, catching snatches of the sea as they drew closer. Jun wanted to drive too and she let him, on a safe stretch of land. They went to the cliff's edge and stayed till the sky was dark. Jun was still in the driving seat. He said, suddenly, that his mother was ill. Runa didn't reply. Most of the time she tried to forget that he had a family. But he went on, *I don't know what's wrong with her*. She could hear his voice now, the fear and need for reassurance. She'd said that she was sorry and asked if it was serious. *Don't know*. He then looked ahead over the cliff and his expression lightened.

"I could drive this car forward and we'd probably die."

"Don't do that, Jun."

"I'm not going to. You're funny. You're suddenly talking like a teacher."

"I am one."

"I know, but you never act like one. You're just funny. Can we go and get something to eat? I'm hungry."

"Yes, but let me drive now."

They switched places. Runa tried to reverse the car but it didn't go into reverse. They shot forward and stopped within a meter of the cliff's edge. Jun grasped the dashboard, looked terrified. Runa smiled. *Don't worry, Jun. I'll get it right this time.*

And she did. The car moved slowly back over crunching sand. She knew that nothing would go wrong because Jun was there and she had to protect him. If she'd been alone, she might well have plunged the car over the cliffs and been killed.

Jun rested his head on her shoulder as she drove back to the main road, one hand tucked gently under her thigh. They stopped at an American all-night restaurant. He didn't mention his mother again.

If she was ill then, Runa thought, she would be much worse now that the affair must have been splashed across the papers.

Lines formed around her, lengthened, shortened, disappeared, and re-formed. She found a plastic orange seat in the waiting area and took out her travel documents. Ticket, fax showing confirmation of her one-night hotel reservation in Shanghai, passport. She also found a coffee-shop discount card, some receipts, and a karaoke-club membership card. None of these things would help her if she didn't find Ping.

She flicked open the passport. Nanao's picture caught the sun so that only her hair showed up. Runa cupped her hand around it to cut out the light. It was a poor photograph. Nanao was grimacing and there was a look of certainty in her expression that Runa had never seen before. It didn't look much like her. Her forehead was crumpled and creased but should have been smooth and clear, like Runa's. Her straight, high eyebrows looked low and heavy. It didn't look much like either of them. When Nanao and Runa were small, people said that they were like two halves of a cucumber. They were sisters, not twins, but similar enough, Runa thought, to confuse the officials. Officials never checked properly. When she imagined Nanao looking for it, her skin burned. For all Runa knew, Nanao might have planned a holiday or have some overseas conference to attend. Runa should have asked. Nanao may not have needed it and may have said yes. Except, Runa thought, that Nanao would never break the law, would never break any little rule.

She wondered if anyone was looking for her. The reporters would not simply lose interest on hearing she had run away. They would be keener than ever. But, if they searched her room, they would see that she had not taken her passport and would search only in Japan. She knew that her affair with Jun was scandalous, but she didn't know if it was illegal. She would lose her job, perhaps never find another one, but could she go to prison? How was she supposed to know these things? Was there a book of rules somewhere that everyone else knew about?

While carrying Nanao's passport, Runa would be Nanao. She would behave as Nanao would so as not to draw attention to herself, so as not to get into more trouble. She unbraided her hair and let it fall over her shoulders. She peered into her compact mirror with a serious, intellectual expression, imagined she was Nanao. She looked like Runa.

A woman's voice came over the speakers, unclear as though she had slipped into the sea and was speaking underwater through a tube. Runa didn't hear what the voice said but people around her surged toward a large door. Children pushed past her knees and she swayed as though she were already out there. So it was time to escape. Her legs wobbled as she walked. It was like a teenage dream coming true. An adventure. And at the end of it, Ping, her best-ever teenage friend.

Ten

Ralph descended in the hotel elevator. His suitcase stood beside him and his money belt was strapped around his waist. The elevator was small but quite grand with wooden walls, glinting mirrors, a floor of dusky pink tiles. The lighting was pinkish too, so that his reflection appeared smooth and rosy. He thought he might be considered quite handsome in the elevator. A shame there was no girl to push the buttons and share the sight of him.

The doors opened on the ground floor and he strode into the lobby, resolved not to look into another mirror today but to keep the image from the elevator in his mind until bedtime. He left his suitcase with the receptionist and headed for the business suite. He was starting to like the hotel, now that he had to leave. The staff was friendly and he knew his way around. Everything was clean. He noticed that the receptionist disinfected the desk pen every now and then, even running the cloth along the chain that connected it to the desk. The shut-

tle bus would depart in half an hour so he could check his email
one last time. Li Hua had already agreed to see him but he
wanted to be sure that she hadn't changed her mind about
coming to meet him at the port.

There were two new messages. One from Barry, saying that
the weather was worse—non-stop wind and rain—and he
didn't mind calling a builder to look at Ralph's roof. The other
was from Li Hua.

Dear Ralph Turnpike

   I look forward to meeting you. Please send me your photo-
graph before you come here. I want to see you. It will be very
nice. I gave you my photograph before. I hope you like it.
   Li Hua

By this evening he would be at the port in Kobe, ready to set
off for Shanghai. It was too late to send a photograph and just
as well. It wouldn't help him. In front of a mirror, with a kind
shade of light, he was sure he had no reason to be ashamed. But
in photographs he never looked quite right. It wasn't that there
was anything wrong with him—certainly not from an Asian
woman's perspective, because he was tall and slim with fairish
hair—but because he was too conscious of the person with the
camera. He looked tense, severe. His mother had always told
him he had a coat hanger in his shoulders in pictures. She used
to make him lean against things—trees or walls—to appear
more relaxed, though it never worked. Li Hua could judge
when she met him and he would do the same for her. He would
be a gentleman and forget her picture—perhaps her mother

had had something to do with it—and wait to see her in the flesh.

He replied to Barry's message.

Don't fix the roof. Don't do anything about it. I'll sort it out when I get back.

The bus arrived on time. Ralph boarded it and worried about his roof for the whole journey. Perhaps he should have put a couple of exclamation marks in to make his message clearer. He really didn't want Barry, or anyone, going into the attic. It was his private place. It was where he kept his private things. He wouldn't want anyone rooting around up there.

Eleven

Runa was the last person to board the ferry. Her legs felt soft and weak, like plasticine. What if she never found Ping? What would she do in China on a stolen passport with a tourist visa, little money, and no friends? And yet she couldn't stay in Japan and become the whore who abused a schoolboy, because she couldn't deny anything but didn't feel guilty. She had always thought it would be interesting to be famous or notorious, but not like this. And she remembered Kawasaki's words—*I'd wring her neck*—and felt sure that he would.

So she picked up her bag, carried a can of Coke from which she sipped as she walked, and crossed from rough concrete to water. Almost immediately it seemed she was lost in a crowd of ecstatic, waving people, unable to see the sides of the deck for arms, legs, and suitcases. She stood still in the middle, absorbed the chaos. She kept drinking the Coke in small cold sips. She was not Runa; she was Nanao. The boat dipped and rose. She felt a little nauseous. That was good. Runa never got seasick but Nanao always did.

BOOK II

Twelve

There was nothing wrong with seasickness pills. They hardly counted as medicine. Even if you didn't take them, you felt better having them in your pocket. The floor lurched as Ralph pushed the cabin door, and he wished he hadn't thrown away the packet before taking even one. It was an accident. When he'd stood at the water's edge and decided to drop his other pills into the sea—to show that he didn't need them anymore—he'd chucked the wrong container, the packet instead of the bottle. It was a bit stupid but sometimes little things confused him. Sometimes he allowed stress to get in the way of noticing. The pills were supposed to stop the stress but they didn't work well. His body seemed to have got used to them, because they didn't have much effect. It was his heart that was sick, ever since Apple, and he was on his way to healing it. But if he hadn't thrown the other pills away he might have taken one and he would be fine now instead of having this uncertain nausea, the feeling that his body may screw up at any second, then explode.

His throat was contracting involuntarily and saliva filled his mouth. He swallowed repeatedly, breathing deeply between gulps.

He put his suitcase on the floor, glad to be rid of it for a while. He had been swapping the case from arm to arm all the way from the port building and now both his elbows ached. A big framed rucksack would have been more practical but he'd felt it would make him look like a student—a mature student—and he wasn't one. Rucksacks always looked dirty, even clean ones.

The cabin was a dark little box with two bunks and a few cupboards. He rubbed a finger down the side of the wardrobe. It seemed clean. In the corner was a door leading to the bathroom. His cabin-mate had already chosen the top bunk, slung a jacket over the pillow, piled sports magazines beside it. Ralph sat underneath wondering if the man would come to introduce himself, what he would be like. He took more deep breaths. *Steady, Ralph, steady.* If there had been single cabins he would have been happy to pay more. He hoped the man didn't snore, or have a cold, or leave hairs in the shower, or walk around naked. People should take care to be considerate of others, but of course they never did.

He swung his legs, checked his watch. The time meant nothing. It wouldn't mean anything for two days. His next appointment was his arrival in Shanghai and he had no control over that. He looked through his cabin-mate's magazines. Young muscular baseball players in action shots, tanned, with taut, compact limbs. The writing was all in Japanese or Chinese. While he was in Tokyo, someone in the hotel lounge had explained how to tell the difference between the two written languages but he'd forgotten. Or hadn't been paying attention in the first place. Ralph wished he had brought some books to read. He reached into his case for *Eastern Blossoms* and flicked through pages that were already familiar to him, then threw the catalog down. The pictures of the girls' faces depressed him. They were so pretty, like Apple, and not at all like Li Hua.

It was funny that after forgetting Apple quite successfully for more than two years, she was suddenly hanging around again, like a ghost. It was as if she didn't want him to be happy with another woman. She was getting into his thoughts so that she could control him as she used to. Next she'd be wanting money to spend, somewhere out there. Good luck to her. He would marry again and that was that.

And he would read the catalog, too, in his own good time, but not now with Apple looking over his shoulder. To make the time pass, he could take a pill—since he still had the bottle— or he could try and make new friends. He went back along the corridor and up on deck to join the crowds.

People were shouting goodbyes across the short stretch of water, being hysterical, and making him feel worse. He loitered awkwardly at the back of the crowd as if he were in a packed bar, waiting for service. Above his head, colored streamers curled in the breeze and fell to shouts and cheers. The wind blew his hair back from his face. Instinctively he pulled it forward, smoothed it down, tasted salt on his lips.

Goodbye, Japan. He thought of the women he'd met there. If the agency had done a better job he could be flying home now, ready to start a new life. Instead, he was still traveling, still searching, carrying dog-eared catalogs and photographs, Internet printouts.

Chunks of writing were printed on his mind.

The Thai women are shy but very warm. Your Thai princess will smile gently and encouragingly when you talk to her. She wants to hear about you. But remember to ask her about herself too. You should ask her how her day has been, or if she saw anything interesting in the shops. This will let her know how SPECIAL you think she is. A Thai woman will not put herself forward too much, so you don't have to worry that she will monopolize the conversation. She is waiting for you to take the lead. SO ENJOY IT!

He should have charged Apple for all his travel expenses and for wasting his time. He had given her everything and was prepared to give more. He would have given her the world if she hadn't betrayed. He rubbed his temples. Since it was Apple's fault that it went wrong, there was no reason why it wouldn't work this time with Li Hua. She wasn't even from the same country.

Ralph took his own ad out of his pocket, a little crumpled and thin. The words were fading but gave him comfort still. It had appeared in several Asian magazines and on the Internet. In a small way, he was famous.

Hi! My name is Ralph. I am a reserved and gentle person. I have a lot of interests. I have my own shop selling art supplies and a

large four-bedroom house which I have enjoyed decorating and
working on in many differing ways. It also has a garage. I have
a BA (Hons) from a prestigious university and I enjoy sketching
in my spare time, especially mountain scenes, gardens and still-
life in general. Although I can, on occasions, become emotional
about things that move me, I see this as a positive aspect of my
character. I don't have any pets at the present time but if you
wanted to have a little cat or dog to keep you company, that
would be all right by me. I am very sensitive and I am not afraid
to say that I need to be loved. I am like a fruit tree that needs the
sunshine and water of a woman's love.

He'd been unsure of the last line when he wrote it but now, in
print, he was rather pleased with it. He was a romantic after all.
He did believe in love. He'd added later, in pencil, *I am a SPE-*
CIAL person. And later still, *both when I'm on medication AND*
when I'm not.

He knew he was kind and gentle. Apple told him that before
she turned on him. She was smiling at the time. It seemed like
a pretty, loving smile, but he didn't know then what lay behind
it. He said to her, "Your smile is very beautiful."

She seemed to like it so he went a bit further.

"Don't ever lose your beautiful smile, darling."

He traced it with his finger. And she'd kept smiling but it
stopped looking like a smile. It was sort of fixed and hard. A
frown or grimace but in the shape of a smile. Maybe she hadn't
understood what he meant. Her English wasn't very good
(though sometimes he thought they pretended about that because he knew that they all studied English at school in Thai-

land). Not that he could speak French, or anything else he learned at school, but that was different because he could already speak English, the International Language.

Try to use a very SIMPLE selection of words. If you say a complicated sentence, the ladies will not understand you. If you ask them, "Do you understand what I'm saying?" the Asian women will ALWAYS say yes but most of the time they don't understand.

He tried that with Apple but it didn't work. She understood him when she wanted to and misunderstood him when it suited her. If he said, we're going out this evening at eight, she would come home from the shops or cinema at nine or ten and act as if she hadn't understood. When he tried to tell her that her cooking was too spicy, she pretended to understand but continued to give him inedible food until he had to make something separate for himself. He wasn't a fussy eater but he simply couldn't manage food so hot that it hurt his mouth. He believed her at first—her innocent surprise and dismay that she had got it wrong—but he noticed that she understood the television, the soap operas, and the news. She watched comedies and laughed in the right places. She understood Ralph when he said, *I'm going out now.* She could barely keep the joy from her eyes. All he'd asked for was love.

He must fall in love with Li Hua. He must have all the things he couldn't have with Apple. Walks by the lakes together, picnics, perhaps a dog. Candles and simple food, a calming voice and touch. Soft hands to bathe him, a sponge of warm water squeezed down his back. A malleable body that would arch weakly beneath his, whisper sweet words into his ear. Cute, funny English that he would understand but that wasn't perfect. Just a little further to go. He was almost there.

Goodbye, Apple. Li Hua is the one. When I put my mind to it, I get what I want. *I get what I want, that's right, Ralph. And let no one deny it.* He looked down at the grey puckered water and all he could think of was that somewhere buried deep and swirling in all that foamy liquid was his packet of seasickness pills.

He didn't care to be outdoors for long when there was nothing to see. He wasn't keen on the sea, too much of it, too cold. No bearings once you were away from the land. But he needed air or he would be sick. He opened his mouth wide until his jaw cracked. Then he inhaled as if to suck in the whole sky and swallow it up. Now, he thought, how am I going to last here for two and a half days? Who shall I talk to first? Who will be my friend?

Thirteen

She grasped the edge with both hands and leaned over, imagined she was falling. The wind battered her face and bit into her ears. Her throat filled with knives of icy air. If she jumped now, she'd never have to make an impossible decision again. It would be so easy. She was worried about Ping. Ping might have changed, might have straightened out. She could be married with children and want nothing to do with her. Runa would have to think of a back-up plan before arriving in Shanghai. She had two days. She couldn't speak Chinese and she didn't know the city. She had enough money to last a few weeks, but without friends she wouldn't survive longer and she couldn't bear to be alone. Runa looked down at the water and started to cry. She couldn't hear her voice and that made her cry harder. She was disappearing, intentionally or not.

She pulled herself back to catch her breath. It would be simple to jump headfirst now and disappear, but not much fun. She only had to look at the creasing black water to know she'd never do it. She must put her faith in Ping. In a few days she would have a new life. She had always found ways of getting into things, getting out of things. It was her specialty and at least she could comfort herself with that knowledge.

At the school, when her life was in danger of standing still, she would go out at night and make things happen to move it on, like stepping onto a treadmill until it was moving forward, then hopping off again. Could she do that now?

There was the time she had gone into a bar in the nearest big town to find friends. She had just split up with Kawasaki because he had started training the baseball team and was at school from six every morning until late in the evenings for practice and on weekends, too. She only spent time with him in typhoons or heavy snow. Even worse, he frightened her by talking about marriage. It was bad enough to think of spending her life with a man she never saw, but out there in the countryside, she would have no other friends. She liked him, but not that much. The whole thing had become dull—no parties, no fun—so she told him it was over but realized from his reaction that it made no difference to him. He started dating Ms. Kuroyanagi a few weeks later. He was about to turn thirty and probably felt it was time to marry so he was looking around for someone who would do.

After that the nights were lonely. She had hardly seen him during her waking hours but at least he had been there when she slept. She couldn't see how she would have a life at the school and started to think she would die there. How did she make it work? Too lonely to sleep, she needed to meet someone who wasn't another teacher. She cycled off to the town and stopped at the first bar she had never been to. A young man was drinking alone and she went to talk to him. She pulled up a stool and filled his glass from the bottle on the table.

"What are you reading?"

"It's about rocks."

"That doesn't sound very interesting."

"I suppose it's not. My boss is interested in stones and stuff. He collects them."

"Is that why you're reading it?"

"He always talks about rocks when we go out drinking. I thought that if I learned some stuff, I might be able to join in, you know, just say something every now and again that didn't sound stupid."

"Sounds like he's the one with no brain. Conversations about rocks? Over drinks?"

"He's not so bad. He's a very good boss. He's done a lot for me. I just want to solve this problem with conversation. I want to become a better employee. Anyone would do the same."

"I certainly wouldn't. I'd rather not have too much in common with my boss. I don't want to end up respecting him. Don't you feel bad drinking that in front of me?"

"Sorry. What would you like? The same?"

"No. A scotch please."

He laughed. "On the—? Oh dear, no. I don't even want to think about rocks now." The barman brought Runa's scotch and she tipped back her head to enjoy the first mouthful.

"It tastes good."

"You drink fast. You must be strong. Very strong."

An hour later, he was doing nothing to help things so she

asked him to come home with her. He looked as if he wasn't sure—perhaps he was married and had a conscience—so she put her hand on his.

"I'll pay," she said.

"It's all right. I paid for those while you were in the ladies'."

"No, not the drinks." Her lips felt dry but she couldn't back down. "I'll pay however much it is that people pay."

He stared at her, open mouthed. "I don't know about that. I don't know about that."

And he kept saying it, even after he had ordered another drink. He wouldn't say no, though, so Runa waited for an answer until she grew bored and just a little embarrassed. Then she left and cycled home alone. She knew now that she could ask; it was in her vocabulary. A few nights later, the same proposition worked perfectly easily with a different man, a waiter in a pizza restaurant. She found that waiters were more likely to say yes. It wasn't a long-term solution to being alone but it helped.

If only, she thought, all men could be waiters, air stewards, bellboys. Dressed, trained, and presented to serve, with politeness and a smile.

Was that before or after Jun? It must have been before. She hadn't realized until now that she even cared for men in uniforms. She laughed, and she knew she must laugh about Ping, too, if she was going to survive this journey. Ping was a good friend, and friends were for life. She'd heard someone say so in a speech contest. She should have tried the phone number again. Ping's handwriting wasn't clear and the sevens might have been fours or nines.

If Jun were here now, he'd be making her laugh. They'd be running around, playing hide and seek on the boat. He would have to find the highest place, the darkest corner. He would be thrilled to travel so far by ferry. For Jun Ikeda it would be a fantastic game and Runa would enjoy every minute with him. She missed Jun but at least the thought of him reminded her that there would be others.

She touched the ends of her hair. *I must remember. I am not myself. I am my sister. Nanao would not behave in such a manner. Nanao doesn't give herself to anyone. But, Nanao, what in the world would you do right now?*

Fourteen

If she can't cook, there is no reason to be disappointed. There are many good cookery courses and she will enjoy the opportunity to make friends with other housewives. And, of course, if she tells you she is not good at cooking, it may not even be true. The Asian women are modest about their many accomplishments. It is one of their endearing charms.

She was a small figure on the ship's deck. Her back was rigid against the wind. Ralph shuddered in the cold, cowered near the doorway, and stared at the woman who looked down at the water. Damp, long black hair blew in seaweed strands. She could be Japanese, Chinese, he didn't know. He had not come out here looking for anyone or anything but now he was excited as though he had found things he had been searching for.

Her hair fell back off her face and he caught a glimpse of her profile. She looked a little like the way he had imagined Li Hua to look before he saw the photograph, and a little like the girl in the elevator. She looked nothing like Apple and yet she was beautiful. This woman looked, somehow, as if she didn't care to be spoken to, acted as if she owned the whole night. But it might be her Asian modesty, that made her seem so. He was fascinated and a little jealous. She was a lovely star in the night, he thought. He could tell her that. *You are shining like a star above the boat, above me.* What a compliment it would be. He wanted to know her name.

As he pushed his right leg to take a step toward her, he was stopped. A loud crash from behind started his legs trembling. A hoarse voice shouted in a foreign language. Ralph jumped around to see a man running across the deck, pursued by another. Their words came out and were eaten up by the wind so quickly it was a wonder they were able to understand each other. What Ralph could tell from the fragments of sound left in the air was that the words were vicious. The taller man reached the edge and stopped, breathless. The other came and shoved him hard against the metal. He slumped to the floor, perhaps to save himself from being flipped over into the sea. He put his hands feebly in front of his face to shield a rain of sharp kicks to his head. He managed to pull himself up again for long enough to grab the shorter man's legs, pull him down. They fought, rolling over and over, now without voices.

Ralph was excited by the violence, so unexpected. The thrill prickled down his spine. He wanted to see—not pain or blood—but grinding force and a blood-red wash of color behind his eyelids when he blinked.

He watched as the woman lurched toward the fighting bodies and shouted at them. She pulled at the shoulders of the shorter one. Ralph stepped back. Brave, he thought, for such a slight girl. The man did not turn on her but calmed for a second, said something gently and politely. It looked to Ralph as if he were saying, "It's all right. Just give us a minute to sort this out. Don't worry about us. We'll be fine." The tall man opened his mouth and shrieked in anger, presumably demanding an end to the fight, but the other kicked his head, again and again, as if driving a tent peg into the ground. The woman's body tensed with each strike.

She looked around for help, noticed Ralph in the shadows, lurking. He stepped forward, sheepishly. He couldn't very well stand there doing nothing.

"Looks nasty," he shouted, hoping she couldn't speak much English.

"Help me."

She seemed frightened. She needed him, and he wanted to put an arm around her. A fight was something beautiful in itself, but with a scared woman upset at the sidelines, it was more gorgeous still.

"Don't you worry," he said, rolling up his sleeves slowly, having no intention of involving himself. He wasn't very well, after all. He hadn't found his sea legs yet. These men would knock him to pieces. His glasses might fall off, might get broken.

But as they turned toward the fight, the two men picked

themselves up and disappeared through the door. It shut gently and firmly behind them.

It was quiet as if they were never there. Just the sounds of the engine and the sea.

"I'm a bit peaky," he said. "Or I would have sorted them out. They seem to have made up, though. Are you very afraid? Did that frighten you?"

She returned to the side and watched the water, rocking gently with her arms wrapped around herself.

"It's chilly," he said, walking over. His voice wobbled in the wind and disappeared. He wasn't sure that she had heard. He was not quite sure he had heard it himself. Ralph looked down, where her gaze was fixed, on the sea's swell. The lights on the side of the ferry caught the swirls of water and made him woozy again. When he looked further out at the black water, waves of terror washed over him. He kept his sight close to the boat and then he could look. He tried to see the water through her eyes, see what exactly she was watching. Little wedding dresses lighting up on a dance floor, one by one, then slipping back into the dark. She glanced at him but didn't speak. There was probably nothing to say in response to his inane remark. Of course it was chilly. He wondered how much English she knew. It was better that she wasn't fluent but she would need a little bit. Apple hadn't been able to say much at first—she'd relied on the interpreter when they met—but when she got to England she found ways of expressing herself, mostly by scowling.

He tried again.

"Would you like my jacket?"

She was small enough to look sweet with a man's jacket swamping her shoulders. It wasn't the same as a woman actually wearing men's clothes, which was, to Ralph, unattractive, no better or more natural than a man wearing women's clothes.

"No, thank you."

She shivered. She faltered as she spoke but Ralph caught a hint of American in her accent and was disappointed. She might be very Westernized. He moved a little closer. His queasiness faded as air filled his lungs and he grew more used to the sight of the sea.

"Where are you from?"

"Japan."

"I've just been in Japan. On business. What with me being a businessman." Of course he had been in Japan. The boat had sailed from Kobe.

"Tokyo, and places. Where do you live?"

"I live in Japan."

So she didn't speak much English. She probably had an American teacher at school but had forgotten everything she learned. He would teach her.

The girl's skin was moon-pale. He thought that if he tried to pry her fingers from the railing, they would snap. He wanted to get her indoors and warm her back to life. But she was looking out at the sky or the sea. He couldn't tell which. He noticed that she wasn't wearing any rings so she couldn't be married.

"I'm a little worried about you."

She turned and nodded in his direction but didn't look at him.

He would give up. He would respect her modesty. He would leave her alone, for the moment, but he would get her name first.

"I'm Ralph. My name's Ralph and I live in England."

She took no notice but didn't seem annoyed. Serene, he thought and said the word again inside his head because he liked it. He wanted her name.

"You are . . . ?"

"Nanao." She said it quickly and firmly, almost before he had finished the question, as if it were information she wanted him to have. Odd, but he didn't know why. He was freezing. He headed across the shiny deck for the door to the warmth of the boat. He would find a table tennis partner, play for an hour or two, and then he'd go to the cafeteria for dinner. But he would seek her out the next day. Nanao. They would be on the boat together for two more days. At the agency you got about ten minutes with each woman, if you were lucky.

He shook his head. Compared with Apple she was an angel. She was exactly what he had been looking for and so much more promising than Li Hua. What was that line about her being a star in the night? If only he could remember it. But he must say something more.

"Are you traveling alone?"

She looked confused. Perhaps it was too soon to ask. "Yes," she said after a moment. "I do."

That was good. He could forget plain Li Hua and rotten

Apple for two days. He would concentrate on Nanao. And if he failed (he wouldn't), Li Hua would still be there. Life was good. Traveling was good. It was something men did, needed to do, connected with discovery and marking territory, and genes. Probably his ancestors had traveled, helping to chart the world and build the empire. Now he was here to represent them. He had made his mark in Thailand and Japan. Now he was off to conquer China.

Fifteen

Runa shuffled irritably along the blue carpet. She shouldn't have woken up. The brutality of the fight had left her shaky. Her head ached and she didn't want to look at the people she passed, couldn't walk too close to another person. She was afraid that somehow the violence had infected her and someone might hit her, or that she would lash out and thump some stranger. She was angry with the two men for hurting each other but she was also worried and couldn't help but pity them. She saw them rolling over and over on the deck, blood shining on their hands and faces. She could still hear their cries above the wind and sea and she wanted to cry.

Runa had only once hit a person and she could remember exactly how it felt, though it was years ago when she was a teenager. She and Ping had been doing some compensated dating, of a kind. They would arrange to have sex with a man in return for jewelry or whatever they felt like that day (Ping had a taste for designer purses), but they would avoid the sex by taking the goods first and running away. If the man chased them, they would scream until he disappeared. But one man didn't give Ping what he'd promised. He understood that she wasn't planning to hang around so he walked out of the love hotel lobby. Ping felt cheated so she ran after him and Runa went too, to protect her. They followed him to his house and Ping threatened to tell his wife unless he gave her money. He told them that he wasn't married and shoved Ping out of the way, cracking her head against the wall. Ping went crazy. She started screaming and hitting him all over his face and chest. He pushed her again. Runa came behind him with a brick and hit him over the top of his head, not very hard.

It was his own fault but Runa had felt so sorry for him, standing with his hand on his head looking utterly lost and confused. She wanted to hit him again and put her arms around him at the same time. She wasn't keen on older men after that. It was all too violent and confusing. Apart from Kawasaki, who was a couple of years older, she dated only younger men.

She lay back on her futon and felt warmth creep into her limbs. The room was large and there was space for ten or more people on the tatami. Runa was glad she had not paid for a proper bed in a cabin. She wanted more people around her tonight. Being Nanao wasn't easy. She had thought it would be; she thought it would mean being sensible, being quiet, not doing much, but now she had to pretend she didn't speak English. Until she saw the English man, she hadn't thought about language. Perhaps it wouldn't matter—most people on the ferry would speak Japanese, Chinese, or both—but she shouldn't identify herself as someone who might be an English teacher. Her head pounded as if it were being kicked. She pressed her fingers into her temples. For now the school and its teachers didn't exist. They didn't exist because she couldn't see them.

Soon only her fingertips and toes were cold. She should eat or drink. Then she would have to find something to do, otherwise she would lose her mind. Perhaps with a little company she could stop dreaming and fill her head with something new.

She found herself thinking again of the man who was being beaten up on the deck. His face was the more aggressive of the two. She'd like to put one finger over his lips to quiet and calm him. In fact, she'd like to see him tonight but she would not do what Runa always did. She was Nanao. Nanao didn't go around picking men up when she needed them. Somehow she already had them. Before she met Hiroshi, she had boyfriends, but each lasted for a long time and they seemed to slide so easily into her life, as if presented on trolleys. Runa didn't have boyfriends as such; she had encounters. She didn't know how Nanao used to do it, how she got them without having to catch them in the first place.

Runa could only behave the way she felt Nanao would and that meant being responsible and practical. She must first have something to eat. After that she would find a place to sit and check out the other passengers. Then she must sleep. She could sleep for the whole journey. She must forget about the man.

She climbed a flight of stairs and felt a burst of excitement. *I'm on a boat, Nanao. I wish you were here with me. Have you heard yet, that I've run away?*

Sixteen

He saw the back of her, sharp-boned and sleek, disappear through the door to the lounge. He couldn't help following. Her long skirt swished around her ankles as if it were freshly laundered and ironed, but her hair was slightly ratty, criss-crossing over itself, from the wind. She moved so lazily, as if to a slow music, but also quite deliberately; she knew where she was going. As Ralph approached the door, he almost expected not to find her on the other side. She seemed likely to turn invisible on a whim and reappear behind him, walk through walls, open her mouth and make the noise of the sea. She would entice Ralph with her beauty and lead him—where?

He paused outside the lounge. Entering a room full of people having fun together was daunting. He didn't want to go in and be stared at, or be left out of whatever they were doing. He couldn't quite see inside, so turned his head sideways and tried to listen. A middle-aged couple appeared in the corridor. Ralph tagged on behind them and entered the smoky room. When he

inhaled, though his nose was tickling already, he found the cig-
arette-tasting air intense and arousing. Its pungency twisted the
atmosphere like the dimming of lights.

In the center of the lounge a young couple was playing a fe-
rocious and rhythmic game of table tennis. A woman sat on the
floor by the table legs, reading a book and occasionally picking
up the ball and bouncing it back to them, expressionless.
Around the edges of the room at round tables people played
cards, chatted, drank, stared ahead doing nothing. Their voices
together formed a low murmur as if all the separate clusters of
people were involved in one conversation. So far Ralph had
not seen a single other white person.

He glanced around for Nanao. She was in a corner with her
back to him. Her head was resting on her hands, bent slightly
forward, and it looked as though she was in deep thought. The
more he watched her, the more he knew she was his. There
were no empty tables. He could either turn around and walk
out, or join another group. There was a spare chair at Nanao's
table. Did he dare? He walked over, pulled out the chair, and
opened his mouth to ask if he could join her. But she was
asleep. A couple of people were watching him so he sat quickly
and fumbled in his pockets for something to look at. He sat for
an hour, watching her over the top of his hotel reservation fax,
as she breathed and dreamed, waiting for her to awaken. The
table tennis continued in the background like a metronome.
Eventually the game ended, the couple put down the paddles.
Nanao woke with a jerk. The sudden quiet must have disturbed
her. She looked at Ralph and jumped slightly.

"Hello again," he said. "I didn't realize it was you, with your head down."

She looked confused but smiled politely.

"I was just going to ask . . ."

She stared at him, ran her fingers through her hair with mild annoyance at its messiness.

"I was just going to ask if you fancied a game of table tennis."

"Pardon?"

"Table tennis." He pointed at the game and mimed a paddle hitting a ball. "Me and you. Play game together. It's fun."

It seemed odd to be playing table tennis on top of water. Of course, there was the boat holding everything up, but still it wasn't quite natural. That was the sort of observation he couldn't make to Apple. She would have sneered. Sometimes he hadn't even been able to think in front of Apple, in case he voiced his thoughts by mistake and she stomped off. *Shut your face you fuck off I don't like you.*

Ralph was better than he expected to be but perhaps that was because Nanao was so astonishingly bad. Each time he served, she lunged the wrong way or simply waved the paddle too high or too low to hit the ball. When she did manage to make contact with the ball, as often as not she sent it flying backward over her shoulder. She was constantly bending down, twirling around, looking for the ball in the wrong place. He kept serving and, occasionally, they managed a short rally. No longer mysterious and aloof, she was now giggly and goofy, a funny uncoordinated child.

"I still asleep," she said, picking herself up from the floor, laughing.

"Never mind!" Ralph caught her serve and rapped it over the net. "We're just playing for fun. And it is fun."

They returned to their table. The couple who had played before them were there and made to move but Nanao pulled over two more chairs to join them. They spoke to Nanao, presumably in Japanese, and Ralph was bored. He stared at his hands. The couple were drinking beer from a vending machine so Ralph bought one for himself and called over to Nanao.

"Something cold to drink? A Coca-Cola?"

She nodded and together they drank. A little later Nanao and the woman were smiling and moving off, cans of drinks in their hands, leaving Ralph alone with the man. Ralph was a little dizzy from the game, and the beer quickly made him lightheaded.

The man was talking to him. Ralph tried to listen. It was all right, really, sitting here with a drink and a man to talk to. Not so different from being in the pub.

"I'm going home to China. I was working in Japan," the man said. "I'm an engineer."

"Me, too. I mean, I was there on business."

"Did you like Japan?"

"Yes. To be honest, I didn't see much. Meeting rooms and a couple of hotels."

"You'll like China better. Where are you going in China?"

"Shanghai. Beijing, perhaps. I don't know."

"You don't know? This is a vacation or business?"

"A vacation. Sort of. I'm meeting someone and then we'll decide where to go."

"Ah, you have a friend. An English friend?"

He was not sure how much he should say, not sure that this was a topic he wanted to move toward. "A Chinese friend."

"That's very good. Your friend will show you everything. Shanghai is a very beautiful city. Your friend will take you all over."

"I hope so."

What would Li Hua do? Would she want to guide him through the city? It would be the romance he had deserved and missed for so long. Walking through a foreign land, hand in hand with his lover. But it wouldn't do to have Li Hua leading him around the place as if she were in charge, just because she knew the place and spoke the language. Ralph must be the leader or they must have a third person—an interpreter or guide—telling him what was what. And, if he did meet Li Hua, he couldn't let her get too comfortable staying in Shanghai because it would not be for long. She'd have to learn that it would stop being her territory, would not be her home, that in England she would learn to live as the visitor. He would be the one on home ground.

In public places you must be assertive and ready to take the decisions. If too many choices are left to her, she may become confused and upset. She is looking for you to be decisive and take her forward. She will respect your leadership and feel safe and protected with you.

Ralph couldn't see how this would work in a city he knew nothing of, where he couldn't read even a street name. It wasn't a problem in Bangkok with Apple because at the beginning they had always had an interpreter. Besides, they were in a hurry and spent only a couple of days together before he flew back to arrange the documents. His heart pumped harder. *Calm down, Ralph. You're not there yet. Li Hua is just an option. You may not even need to meet her. Calm down. Deep breath. Steady.*

"My name is Wu."

"I'm Ralph."

"My wife's name is Mei Ling."

Ralph felt a shock of loneliness. *My wife.* "I used to be married."

"Really?"

"I loved my wife, but she didn't love me. She left me." He paused. He could see that Wu was listening at the same time to a story being told in Chinese at the next table. "As far as I know, she went back to Thailand. But she didn't tell me and she was gone for a long time so I had to divorce her."

"Are you all right?"

"Yes. I'm fine. Never been better."

"You can always get married again."

"I will. Sometimes it doesn't seem easy. Other times it does and I can't wait. You're lucky to be married."

Mei Ling arrived, alone, and spoke to Wu. They left Ralph without saying goodbye.

And, again, he must find Nanao. Drunk, excited, and warm he was sure she had gone back outside where he had first seen her. He opened the door to the deck and looked outside, but she wasn't there. The gap where she had been was filled by nothing because he could see only emptiness in the dark. The sea was calm but wild in its own way just because it was the sea.

How could she like it so much? What was there to stare at? He liked to be outdoors if he was on dry land. A nice hill or mountain. On water, he liked to be indoors. No, best of all he liked to be on his way indoors. He loved closing the door against the wind and feeling the warmth of a carpet under his feet. Comfort, a certain kind of safety.

He realized he had drunk, but he hadn't eaten and was beginning to feel hungry. He went to the restaurant and confronted the array of food. He didn't mind eating foreign food when in Rome and all that, but he wouldn't mind a hamburger and fries. So far, on his travels, he had survived well on fast food for meals and carefully washed fruit from supermarkets, to be sure of an intake of vitamins and fiber. The ferry's restaurant, if you could call it that (the sign above the door did), did not appear to serve hamburgers, or fries.

Ralph walked over to the counter and peered into the metal vats of food. It seemed hygienic but you'd have to check the kitchens to be sure. Different kinds of vegetables, some seafood, and something meaty that smelled of pork but could be anything. He pointed at vegetables and rice, carried them on a tray to a table. He had never been keen on Chinese food and now knew that he was not too good with Japanese either. But whether he married Li Hua or Nanao, that would have to change, at least until she learned to cook properly for him.

He liked to think about the things she could learn, at his guidance. He would pay for her to do a cookery course in England, as his catalog suggested. She might like that. And it would be a good way for her to make some English friends, especially with nice housewives who would provide good role

models. It should be a daytime course so that the other women
wouldn't have jobs. He would arrange for her to have a student
visa. This would give them plenty of time together before they
needed to make wedding preparations. He crunched a piece of
baby corn and washed it down with cold water. The food was
not bad, better than he'd expected.

He returned to his cabin and took a shower. He sloughed
away dead skin, feeling glad that he had paid for a deluxe cabin,
not one of the cheaper ones with as many as eight beds. Hordes
of other people snoring away just meters from him. Or, even
worse, he could have paid less and had a single tatami mat in a
room full of other sleeping bodies. Imagine some calloused foot
stepping on your face in the middle of the night. Or clamber-
ing over bodies and catching your own foot on a warm hairy
stomach. Privacy was not a luxury so he'd paid the top price to
suffer only one cabin-mate.

He scrubbed his face to get rid of the salt, licked his chin to
make sure it had gone. The boat was beginning to rock harder.
They must be some distance away from Kobe, and it was only
going to get worse. He knew that if he could just throw up, he'd
feel better. But he didn't want to let himself. He held it back.
He remembered it from childhood as being painful and somehow alarming, bringing tears. Different from when you were
drunk and just glad to get it out.

He poured shampoo onto his head, rubbed it to a lather, let
the soft white foam slip down his neck and back. He thought of
his new power shower at home, dripping, perhaps, in his ab-
sence. If the water was hot enough and the pressure was powerful, he had read, it should be possible to get clean without

using any kind of detergent. Then you avoided potentially car-
cinogenic chemicals without sacrificing hygiene. This shower
was not quite powerful enough to be sure though, so he rubbed
himself from head to toe in soap.

His mood had faded like the daylight. He was becoming nervous about the girl. How he would love to skip Shanghai and
go straight home. Travel, he now decided was exhausting, re-
lentless. You were never allowed to stop, even when you were
resting in one place. You knew you couldn't stay there and you
were always worrying about what to eat and what was safe to
eat. He imagined the ferry was crossing the English Channel
from Calais to Dover and that he'd soon see the white cliffs,
and Apple was waiting for him in the car. But Apple couldn't
even drive so what was she doing behind the wheel?

He rubbed a little of the lathered soap into his eyes to make
them sting. He was nowhere near home, but he couldn't go
back without his treasure. He thought of Nanao again. You are
going to be mine, he said, because I need you, and you are going
to come home with me. My house, which is a beautiful house,
is all decorated and ready for you. My house awaits you (unless
you have any diseases or infections, but you look so polished
and clean).

He stepped out of the shower, reached for his glasses and silk
cloth. He rubbed the lenses several times but couldn't get them
quite right. He'd had a new pair made with non-reflective coat-
ing so that he'd come over better in interviews at the agencies.
Barry had told him that his old glasses were too shiny and over-
magnified his eyes. That was all very well, but it was impossible
to get these quite as clean as his old ones. Instead of having

glasses that reflected and glinted, he now had ones that were always slightly smeared.

He took his towel—soon he would not have to perform these tasks for himself—and dried the spaces between his toes, one by one, carefully, imagining that the towel was held by her. Then he lay back and let his arms go around an imaginary shape of her—squeezing her flesh right to her little bones, almost crushing them—until he was hugging himself tightly.

He thought of Nanao curled up in her bed. Nanao. He could imagine her in a kimono with a painted white face like a geisha. Serene, helping him to stay calm, never demanding he be this or that, never judging him. It sounded like n-now the way he said it but it was different from her mouth. He must hear it again tomorrow. He pulled the covers over his head and wished the boat would rock a little harder, wished Nanao's body were under the sheets, her limbs all tangled up with his.

She will be demure in public and will be embarrassed by public displays of affection. But in bed she knows it is an honor for her to pleasure her man. The Asian woman never gets "headaches"!!

It would be good to be *pleasured*. For now he had to pleasure himself.

He shut his eyes, saw his attic, Apple's clothes and the lights. Then the hall, softly lit for the evening.

The front door opens and Apple steps in. He grabs her, pulls her toward him, feels her warm little arms flapping as he tries to show his love. He is throwing her across the hall, surprised and aroused by his own strength. He pulls her around by her hair. She is trying to deny that she has been seeing another man but he knows she is lying. She laughs at him. He screws her on the stairs, on the landing, in the bed-

room, and in the attic. Each time he is a little stronger and she is weaker.

Ralph thrust into the mattress. The bed creaked and when Apple was so weak that she was as good as dead, he ejaculated, grunted, and relaxed forward into a pool of his own liquid.

And with his tiredness came the anger that he could never prevent. Apple may not have had headaches but she gave him one. Sulking, flinching when he held her hand. A little stone in bed. "You finish? You finish?" she would ask. Wrinkling up her face when she thought he wasn't looking, when he was only telling her how much he loved her. He had told her, "you are the *apple* of my eye," and she just nodded as if that were obvious. Later she didn't bother to nod. She learned to say *shut your face* from some daytime soap opera and used every opportunity to prove she understood it. *How's my Apple today? Shut your face. Shall we have some breakfast darling? You fuck off shut your face.* Back then he thought her name was sweet—there were so many good jokes and puns—but now he saw that Apple was a silly name. Her real name, the one she wrote on the forms, was long and difficult with about five syllables. Ralph couldn't remember it. She would always be Apple. Apples would always be her.

But he must look to the future. Apple was gone and good riddance. She hadn't deserved to hang around any longer. Now he had a Japanese beauty and a China doll to choose between. He could play eeny meeny all the way from one country to the other.

As he went to sleep he always saw his house. At the moment it was all locked up, safe. It was a solid square house with four windows on the front and a big door. It was like a face, the kind of house that children draw in pictures. It looked, Ralph thought when he first saw it with an estate agent jangling keys at his shoulder, the way a house is supposed to look and that was why he chose it. The other houses he saw didn't have faces. Before he left for Asia, he fitted special window locks and installed a burglar light in the garden. He called his brother Barry and asked him to check up on the place, once a week if possible. He didn't ask Barry to weed the garden, but he hoped his brother would see that as part of the job. It was painful leaving the house. It was hard for him to imagine all the different rooms, so beautifully and recently decorated, without himself inside. And if someone burned it down, or broke in and destroyed the place, how would they find him here on the boat? Then there was the roof. May it not be raining in England now.

He talked to Barry in his head. *Don't fix the roof. There's no need. I'll sort it out when I get back. Never mind a few leaks. No, don't fix it. What? Barry asked. Are you serious? Is it the money? I'd get that roof sorted now if I were you. No, said Ralph. Don't do anything. I'm serious.*

If rain were coming through, the roof would be wrecked. How could he not have checked it before he left? But if anyone went in while he was away, they'd have to go up into the loft. And if they pressed the switch on the stairs to turn the loft light on, they would be putting on the twinkling lights strung across the rafters. They'd think he was mad or they'd laugh at him. He was filled with shame. But he was thousands of miles away and, for now at least, no one could ask him a single question. He was beyond reach.

He was farther from home than he had ever been. He had made new friends, he thought, and was just beginning. He reached onto the bedside table for his wallet and fumbled for the photograph of Li Hua. In the dark, if he squinted, he could just see her face. She looked the same in the dark as she did under light. Plain. A sweet smile, but plain nonetheless. It might be the way her hair was scraped back from her face into a ponytail or braid or something. You couldn't tell what it was, but it wasn't attractive. He rolled over and as he did so, someone on the top bunk moved too. Ralph was not alone. The other sleeper must have been there all the time. A smooth, muscular arm slipped over the edge and hung above Ralph's face. Ralph turned to face the wall.

Don't fix the roof. I'll sort it out. I'll sort it out. He heard his thoughts repeat without any meaning and knew he must almost be asleep.

Seventeen

R una was thinking of Jun. She was awake but almost asleep and was afraid that when she woke up she would be holding on to the body of the woman next to her. She clung to things, people, whatever was there in the night. If she was alone, she sometimes attached herself to the edge of the bed. Kawasaki said that she was like one of those toy koala bears that gripped your finger. She couldn't be sure that she wouldn't roll over in her sleep, fasten herself to the warm, sleeping body beside her. And there was nothing she could do to prevent it. She never knew in advance that it would be the kind of night when she would need to hold someone. She would just wake up to find that it was.

She was trying to remember her last day as a teacher, to remember Jun's face as she saw it on the playing field. But the memory kept flipping over and instead of her last day at school, she saw her first.

* * *

She was cycling into the school entrance, squeezing gently on the brakes. It was a cold afternoon, turning into early evening, and she shivered as the bicycle slowed. Or maybe it was not so cold and she was shivering with nerves. She hadn't intended to be a teacher. After university she was planning to work in a shop until she could think of something better. But she bumped into a family friend one day at a bus stop and, when he heard she had an English degree and was unemployed, he promised to put in a good word for her at the private high school where he used to work. She couldn't say no and then, when they offered her a job, she was obliged to accept it with gratitude and stick it out for a few years so that the family friend wouldn't lose face.

She wore a rucksack on her back and there was something hanging from the handlebars, another bag perhaps. The school drive curled through tall, wispy bamboo and up to the grey blocks. The concrete twinkled as it passed beneath her wheels.

As she put both feet on the ground to stop the bicycle, she realized she was afraid. She hadn't paid much attention to school the first time round and now wished she had spent more time noticing what teachers did to be teachers. But she was interested, too. What she saw in front of her in the dreary school ground was astonishing, like a circus beginning.

She was looking at an array of blue uniforms and tracksuits, all shapes and sizes, running around, practicing tennis, basketball. Some girls—the drama club?—stood in a group on a flight of steps like a family having its picture taken, chanting strange sounds and reciting tongue-twisters. It took Runa a moment to see the heads, arms and legs of the teenagers inside the blue garments. She turned toward the main building. Music came from two boys on the edge of the field, one seated in front of an electronic organ. The other stood in front of him and sang scales to the synthesized accompaniment.

A group of girls with pigtails leapt around in some kind of cheerleading routine. At intervals, they screamed the school name and followed it with an earnest *one two three!* in English. Runa looked for somewhere to leave her bike and when she turned back the cheerleaders had formed a human pyramid in her path. She didn't know what this meant. She smiled, uncertainly she felt, and said hello. The tiny girl at the top bent her knees and with a look of intense concentration, somersaulted to the ground and took Runa's heavier bag. Her expression was serious. She walked alongside Runa to the entrance of the main building. The other girls stared and whispered but not, Runa thought, unkindly. They were curious.

She met the principal and assistant principal in an airless office with vases of almost-dead flowers on the shelves and an electric fan whirring near her ear. She drank a cup of over-stewed tea and signed her contract. Her right hand was a little numb from cycling in the cold air and caught on the paper as she wrote. Then she pressed her wooden name-stamp into a pad of red ink and printed it onto the contract. A man from the school office came to present her with a chalk box. She was waiting to be found out. She didn't feel like a teacher. She was only twenty-four and didn't feel like an adult at all.

The head of English took Runa's bags and led her, silently, across the playing field, behind a row of trees, and over a small road to the teachers' apartments. He switched on the light in the flat and they blinked together in the fluorescence.

It had a nice musty smell, as though no one had lived there for years.

"A little stuffy," the teacher said, almost to himself, and he went to open the window.

There was a small bunch of violets on the table, in a scratched glass tumbler that might have come from the school canteen.

"How pretty. This is lovely."

The man moved to the doorway, nodded awkwardly.

"You must be tired. If you need any more help, don't hesitate to come over to the staffroom. There's usually someone there till ten or eleven at night."

Runa looked out of the window. She could see directly into the main school building. It was dark now except for a long, bright stretch of windows on the first floor. She saw people moving around, conversing, heads bent over desks.

"Thank you for your kindness."

Then it was the next morning. Overnight Runa had turned into a teacher. She was in the staffroom, introducing herself to the rows and rows of people at desks, bowing and promising to do her best. At that point, of course, she hadn't met Jun Ikeda of class 5-7.

* * *

She rolled over, lay on her front, and folded her arms under her head. These memories embarrassed her when she saw how she had behaved afterward. She needed to find Jun inside her memory of the school. She needed to get back into the classrooms. Runa visualized the blackboard, the little desks, her register, tried to recall her first sighting of Jun Ikeda.

She was in the classroom. She had to teach from Ministry of Education textbooks.

Hi, Fred, I'm Hanako.

Hi, Hanako, I'm Fred.

It's nice to meet you, Fred.

It's nice to meet you too, Hanako. Say, would you like to play tennis with me?

Yes, I'd love to. I really like tennis. Tennis is my favorite sport.

Great! Who's that man over there?

That's Mr. Smith. He's a history teacher. He likes tennis, too.

These were the smallest children, the twelve-year-olds. Runa wanted to teach them some real English but she was beginning to forget it herself. And it would never be allowed. It was easy teaching similar dialogues to the ones she had learned when she was at school, but it made for dull lessons.

When that class ended, Runa had to walk to the other side of the school. She had been asked to cover a fifth-year boys' class. As she moved through the corridor, she noticed that the blackboard in each classroom had the same phrase written on it.

Little did I think that it would rain this morning.

Five classrooms in a row, all saying the same thing, like roadside billboards coming up with large slogans. As she passed the first classroom she saw the sentence and thought nothing of it. By the third room she was asking, who is saying it and why did they not think it would rain? And who would be listening to such a sentence. By the time she had reached the fifth room, the one where she would teach, the sentence had become nonsensical.

She felt so strange and dizzy entering the classroom that it took a moment to compose herself in front of the boys. She wasn't used to this kind of energy. She was not used to the smell or feel of the room. In shape and size the room was identical to her first-year classroom, but it felt a different color, a different place because of the older boys. And all through the lesson she was aware that one boy, quiet though seeming confident, watched her closely. She didn't know if she felt good or bad, only that she felt something, intensely. She looked out of the window at the sunshine on the roof of the gym, the girls playing tennis, and wondered how likely it would be to rain. Not very likely, she thought, on such a crisp blue day.

But that boy may not have been Jun Ikeda. She didn't know him then. He could have been any fifth-year boy, excited to have a young female teacher for one lesson. Never mind. She could make him be Jun. She turned the boy in the classroom into Jun, watching her, and felt better. She pulled her bedding close to her skin. Jun Ikeda seemed younger every time she thought of him. Sometimes it bothered her and sometimes it didn't. It was connected with being alone.

She could never help but miss the last person she had slept with.

She opened her eyes, pulled her shoulders back to stretch them. She had been dozing so she sat up to be sure that she couldn't drift off again. Her body was not quite catching up on sleep, but her mind was trying to catch up on dreams, regardless. It was morning. She was lying alone on a crumpled futon, on a boat. The sea was making her mind go soft. She rubbed her forehead. All this rocking made her head hurt.

Around her people came and went, dressing, talking, putting on lipstick and fiddling with lenses in their eyes. They looked like teachers from the school. Each face somehow resembled one she used to see in the staffroom. She half expected to hear the electronic chime, the principal's voice in the corridor. Imagine if they had come after her and were now on the boat. It would be impossible to escape.

Eighteen

She was flicking through the pages of a magazine. It looked like some fashion thing and the models were Western. There was a cup of tea or coffee in her right hand. Ralph stood beside her, wondered whether to sit down or wait to be invited.

"Good morning, Nanao. I trust you slept well."

She looked at him and nodded. Had she understood? He would ask again, to be sure.

"You—sleep well?" He shut his eyes and tilted his head onto his hands to mime sleep. He had a sudden memory of playing a sleeping gnome in a primary-school play and stood upright again, cleared his throat.

"Yes, thank you."

"You like beauty sleep, I think. I—not need beauty sleep. Me no." He laughed.

She smiled. He slid onto the chair opposite. It was going well. She thought he was funny.

"So. Are you going to China for anything nice?"

She thought for a moment, as if trying to find the correct English words.

"My friend. To see my friend."

"Ah. I see. A Chinese friend?"

"Yes." She put the magazine down and was giving him her full attention.

"A boyfriend?"

"No." She shook her head, laughing. "I don't have a boyfriend."

"You're single."

"Yes."

"And what are you going to do with your friend?"

"I don't know." She giggled. "Nothing special."

"A nice trip and then back to Japan."

"Maybe. I don't have plan."

A lady of leisure then. She could be a student, though she didn't seem like the studious type.

"Today is very long," he said. "Today maybe very boring here on boat. You have plans for today?"

"No." She shrugged her shoulders, laughed again. It was a shy, girlish laugh. How could he make her want to spend her day with him? The boat was a romantic place. They had so little time to get to know each other and he mustn't waste it. He had an idea.

"I teach you English. Many English words. You want to learn English with me?"

"Ah." She seemed at a loss for a moment. "No, thank you."

"Just a little? I not want money. I buy you coffee. We have a nice time. Together. You and me."

"Maybe—later."

"Later. That's fine. You find me when you want to learn English. Very useful language. We enjoy ourselves. I look forward to later." He winked and gave a friendly little wave as he left. She waved back and returned to her magazine.

What would he teach her? Things they could say to each other that would lead from innocent conversation to flirtation to, he hoped, bed and marriage. So far he was doing well. He was turning out to be a better flirt than he had thought. If only he'd had the confidence to be like this when he was younger. Flirting, chatting up women. These were things that other people knew how to do, or so he had believed. But in those days he was looking for the wrong kind of woman. It was different now that he knew how to get to the place where the grass was so much greener. But where should their next conversation start?

Your Asian woman will be hoping for security. You should tell her about your JOB and your HOME. There is no need to boast but at the same time it is important for her to know that she is going to be looked after—remember she is giving up the security of her own family and culture to be with you. The least you can do in return is show her that she will be provided for to the best of your abilities.

He would wear his new tie. He would rub at his glasses to get them as clean as he could and he would practice some sentences so that there was no danger of being tongue-tied.

I run the shop for pleasure more than anything else. Of course, making money is a pleasant bonus—and always a surprise—but in the end it's just what I enjoy doing. My house? It's not huge. The third and fourth bedrooms are small, boxrooms really, but it does me well. And I've got a small shed in the garden where I keep my terrible sketches and paintings, along with my garden furniture.

He could try out some different ways of talking about himself to make his successes clear without appearing immodest.

Nineteen

Runa moved around in front of the mirror, checking her image from different angles. No matter how she tried to lose all expression from her face, she looked too intent to be Nanao. Even expressionless, there was something in her face that she couldn't get rid of, something that defined her as being Runa, a kind of hunger, she thought, or just plain badness. There was just too much of herself spilling out from behind her eyes and through her pores. She moved to the back of the changing room to see her face from a distance. Perhaps it wasn't a question of too much of something, perhaps the strangeness was that something was missing.

Nanao had once told Runa she would never be happy. "You want to have everything," she said. Runa had laughed at the time. Everything? If you thought there was a knowable "everything" in the first place, a finite number of things up for grabs, then already your sights were too low. Wanting everything meant wanting nothing very much at all as far as Runa could see. She tried to explain this to her sister but Nanao didn't understand. She was trying out a new kind of mold killer at the time, spraying the solution onto her bathroom wall, scraping pink and blue mold from the grouting as if it were the most interesting thing in the world, hardly listening to Runa at all.

Runa continued to stare at the person in the mirror. Was there something of Nanao behind her eyes? Certainly it didn't feel strange to be called Nanao by the man who kept talking to her in English, who wanted to teach her. She smiled. He had no idea that he would be teaching English to an English teacher. She felt bad lying. After all, he was just a sweet old guy who wanted to talk. He probably had a daughter he missed, but nonetheless she would have to avoid him. It wouldn't be hard. She was planning to have a day doing what Nanao would approve of: keeping out of trouble. She had noticed that there was a communal bathtub with a view of the sea. The bath in the love hotel had somehow left her wanting more and she couldn't think of a nicer, warmer place to be. Perhaps later she would be like Nanao and have some simple, pleasant conversations with strangers.

She stripped off her clothes, took a quick shower, put her hair up with a purple plastic clip she found on the floor. She piled her clothes into a basket and slid it onto a wooden shelf next to another. The other basket contained quilted pyjamas and fluffy socks. The bath was large and rectangular. An elderly woman sat in one corner with her head back, eyes closed. Runa was about to step into the water when she noticed that the woman's features seemed to be settling into a face that she knew but couldn't place. The face had a tiny nose and was flat, so flat, in fact, that you could only see it from the front; there was no profile. Perhaps Runa remembered it from the port. It was a friendly, motherly face. The wrinkles around the eyes showed warmth and humor. It would be good to talk to her, whoever she was. Runa climbed into the bath and the woman looked up, smiling through the steam. The smile was enough to set Runa talking.

"I'm going to see my friend in China. I haven't seen her for years." She realized it was the wrong way to start a conversation, talking about herself, being informative and direct, without any warm-up. But she hadn't spoken properly to anyone for days and just hearing her own voice sounded odd. Talking to the man didn't count because she had only said a few words, they were not in her language, and they were not a reflection of her thoughts.

"You must be excited." The woman nodded gently as she spoke.

"Oh, I am. For years she's been so far-off and hazy, and now that I'm getting closer to Shanghai, I can't believe I'm going to see her. She'll be standing right in front of me, and we'll talk to each other as if we'd never been apart." She shook her head. "It's too much to believe."

"It's important to stay in touch with friends."

"I promised her I would when she left Japan. But then I didn't. She left in a hurry, you see and then I went off to university, not that it's any excuse but . . ." She stopped to cough. The muscles in her throat were beginning to tire.

"Had you known her for a long time?"

Runa swallowed and cleared her throat. "Just a few months.

I suppose it doesn't sound much but at the time we were insep-
arable. It was my last year at high school and I suppose that's an
impressionable age. It is, isn't it? She wasn't a school friend,
though. I met her by chance in the street and we just knew we
were going to be friends. To be honest, I've never had another
friend like her."

"That's a stressful age, university entrance exams and what-
have-you. My son's at high school now."

"It is for most, but not really for me because I didn't study
much. I was supposed to be in my room every evening, working
hard but, you know, I couldn't. I was alone in the house because
my mother was in hospital—she was there for years before she
died—and my father and sister were looking after her. I wanted
to help but they said I should study. They wouldn't let me help
my mother. I hardly saw her till the funeral when, of course, it
was too late."

She stopped again, massaged her neck gently. She remembered the conversations where Nanao and her father thought
they were being so kind to her, saying that they could manage.
"That's right. They wouldn't let me help so I used to go out
after school. There was a huge shopping center not far away
and I always went there. I don't know why. It wasn't as if I ever
had any money."

The woman said nothing. She lay still in the water.

Runa was back at the footbridge. It was just a regular concrete bridge leading from a car park to the shopping center and
beneath was a busy main road. It now seemed a hundred meters
high and longer than the width of any road. Runa used to rest
her arms on the railing and look out at the road and at the grey

buildings on either side, piling up into the horizon. She'd go home with dust or bits of old chewing gum stuck to her uniform.

She was there because she didn't care too much about her exams. She knew that without much strain she would get into an average university, and that would be fine. She had decided on English because there was always the possibility of being an exchange student in Australia or California for a year and lazing on beaches. She imagined bronzed movie-star boyfriends and endless sunshine.

All her friends were studying night and day, so Runa would head for the shopping center, the lights, crowds, piped music. She wandered around looking at clothes and CDs. There was a bookshop with a large magazine rack and she would read her way through the magazines, from teens' to women's, to celebrity gossip, economics, pornography, comic strips. When she had finished she would go to the footbridge and look down on stick-people pushing carts, filling car trunks.

So she was standing there one afternoon, thinking about the day at school, the tedious lessons and the endless sitting and listening that wore her out. As often as possible, she slept in class, just leaned forward over her desk and switched off. In a pool of sunshine, she couldn't stay awake. But when she was out of school, even as she passed through the gates, she was fully alert and full of the late-afternoon air.

And then, Ping showed up.

She ambled along the bridge and stood next to Runa. Her long hair ruffled slightly in the breeze and thin, dry ends flicked Runa's face.

"Cigarette?"

"Thanks."

Runa took one and lit it from the girl's, hoping no one she knew would see her. It was only her second or third cigarette ever. She would have to work hard not to cough.

"I'm Ping. I'm Chinese." Ping smiled broadly. She had wonky eyebrows that made her smile seem crooked. Runa liked it.

"Nice to meet you."

"What's your name?"

"Runa."

"I've been watching you. You come here all the time and just stand on this bridge like you're a signpost or set of traffic lights or something. Don't you have anything better to do?"

"Not really."

"You like it here?"

"I suppose."

"I'm a student. I'm studying Japanese. Do you mind if I practice on you?"

"OK. But you don't sound as if you need much practice."

"Oh, I do. We can go to a café and chat. I haven't got any money though."

"Do you live in Japan permanently?"

"Kind of. Not officially."

"Just here to study, right?"

"Officially." Ping took a drag of her cigarette and exhaled slowly, importantly. "I'm here as a student, but I get up to other things."

"I see."

Runa didn't see, but they began to meet every afternoon. Runa skipped school as often as she dared. Ping never seemed to have classes at college. They wrote love letters together. Runa invented a boyfriend named Takayuki and wrote to him. They chatted for hours. Runa couldn't remember what they used to talk about, but there never seemed to be enough time together. They looked around the shops together, trying on clothes and listening to pop CDs.

But neither had much money, and before long they were shoplifting the items they tried and it seemed so natural they couldn't believe they'd never done it before. Over a few months they had a collection of things they wanted—clothes and CDs—as well as many that they didn't but that were entertaining to steal: vases, a wok, a deckchair. A male shop assistant saw them trying to leave his shop with a wedding dress and chased them until they dropped it and ran away.

They had both developed a taste for things they couldn't afford, but after that were wary of going back to the shopping center to steal, and that was when they started arranging dates with rich men. Runa had no idea now how they came to the decision—it was certainly Ping's idea—and soon they were catching trains into the city at night where they picked up men, promising sex in return for a pair of earrings, tickets to concerts. They agreed that if an attractive man offered, they would have sex, but that never seemed to happen.

One day Ping came to the footbridge to tell Runa that she was leaving. She hadn't paid for or attended her classes for months so her student visa was canceled and she had to leave Japan.

"It's so unfair. I've learned much more by doing it my own way."

"What are you going to do in China?"

"I've already worked it out. I've got a friend who gets Chinese people into Japan using fake conferences and stuff. I'm going to work for him in Shanghai. My Japanese is good enough. I should have come here that way myself. I'm glad I didn't go to my classes, though. We had fun, didn't we?"

"I'll write to you. Give me your address."

"You don't have to. I haven't been a good addition to your life."

"What do you mean?"

"Just that you would have done well in your exams if it weren't for me."

"I don't care. It was my fault, too. I did well enough and I'm going to an OK college. That was all I wanted. We have to stay in touch."

"You'll be going to university and making new friends. I'm not coming to Japan again."

"Please give me your address and phone number."

And Ping scribbled them onto a page in Runa's math exercise book.

Finally Runa was on her way to finding out what had become of Ping. She took another look at the woman. She had closed her eyes again and Runa scrutinized her face, the pores, the little hairs above her top lip. Was she, perhaps, the old lady who had walked past the school when Jun and Runa were on the roof? But that was impossible because it was dark and Runa had only seen her from a distance. Perhaps she was the woman cutting bamboo shoots the night that Runa ran away. Could she be? The woman opened her eyes, saw Runa looking, and smiled. It was hard to tell. Runa registered what the woman had said: *My son's at high school now.* She looked too old to have a high school-aged son. But, if she was following Runa, who was to say that she wasn't Jun Ikeda's mother? Jun had told her his mother was ill so she might have been old.

Now that she was far away, she found herself thinking of Jun more and more. She didn't want to, but he was there. Even when she was thinking about China and what she would do, Jun was still hanging around in the background, being thought about by another part of her brain. No, it was still not love, just thoughts.

The woman watched Runa intently, listening and encouraging her to speak without saying anything about herself. It was strange. Her eyebrows curved and tapered just like Jun's, but she could not possibly be his mother. She wasn't well enough to spy on her son and follow his teacher to another country. It was a crazy idea.

Runa dried herself with a small towel, gazed in the mirror at her reflected naked body. It was perfect. Whatever was happening around her, she was a beautiful young woman, sexy, intelligent, and independent. She could go as far as she wanted. She dressed, loving as always the sensation of pulling clothes over her limbs, letting them settle on her curves. All wrapped up like a present to herself, she unclipped her hair, shook it down her back.

*   *   *

She would seek out the two men who were fighting. Not that she was *so* attracted to one of them—she barely saw their faces—but Nanao would want to check that neither was seriously hurt, that they were not intending to take their quarrel further. Now that she thought about it, so would Runa.

She stepped out of the bathroom, into the narrow corridor that she was tired of seeing. She looked up and there they were, right in front of her. The two men had changed their clothes and were wearing identical soft white T-shirts with jeans. Their faces were bruised and bloodied. One had a black eye and a swollen lip. The other had a gash down his cheek. If it weren't for the specks of dried blood hanging off, Runa thought, the wound would almost be attractive.

"Hello." She stood right in front of them. They stopped and regarded her with surprise.

"Oh. It's you. Hello." The one with the gash smiled, then winced. His eyes were large, black, and shiny. Runa was reminded of some kind of insect.

"I was worried about you."

"Were you? Oh, our fight. Don't worry about that. It was nothing. I've got a bottle of sake in my cabin that was supposed to be a present for my uncle in China, but we've decided to drink it ourselves. This place is so boring, I don't think I can last two more days. How do people stand it? Can you imagine going on a cruise and being stuck on a boat for a week or more? No way. Would you care to join us for a drink?"

"Thanks." She was fascinated.

"I'm Sam. He's Shin. I'm half-Japanese and half-Chinese. But he's completely Japanese."

"I see."

"Come on then. Let's have a drink."

She followed them along the corridor. Already she was forgetting why she was with them. She had recognized them by their bruises but those marks seemed to be fading by the second. At any rate, there she was, falling asleep on her feet. Why was Sam dong all the talking? She wondered why he had an English name.

Sam opened the door. There were two bunks so Runa assumed the pair were sharing a cabin, but it seemed Shin was a visitor too.

"It's very nice," Shin said. "I wish *I* could have afforded a cabin." His expression when he spoke was droopy, pathetic, but when he turned quiet his features set into rough crags, like a face carved into a mountain or cliff.

"Here we are." Sam took a bottle of sake from a bag on the floor. "Aren't there a couple of glasses in the bathroom?" He looked at Shin with impatience. "Go on and find them, then."

Shin, stood, slouching like a teenager, and went to check. He returned with two glasses then went out into the corridor.

Runa remembered the fight and wondered about their relationship.

"Are you related?"

"No. Just friends." He shrugged as though the friendship were something that couldn't be helped. He smiled pleasantly at Runa. Normally she would take this opportunity of being alone with him to flirt a little and see if there was a possibility of knowing him better but she was being Nanao and Nanao would sit politely and not say too much and probably not drink too much sake.

Shin returned with a paper cup. He poured sake into it and the two glasses. He held the paper cup out to Sam who snorted and told him to keep the crappy one for himself. Shin poured himself an extra measure and drank it sulkily. Runa tried to start a conversation.

"I've never been to China before." She thought, if she got on with these men, perhaps she could ask them for help, tell them what had happened to her.

"I have. I've got some relatives there. Mind you, I've only met them once, so really I'm a tourist. Shin's coming with me for fun."

She wondered which of them would be having fun. She turned to Shin and asked, "It's your first visit, then?"

Sam answered for him. "Yes. He can't speak any Chinese so I'll be doing all the work. I'll probably have to pay for every-thing, too, since he doesn't earn any money."

"What do you do?"

Sam allowed Shin to answer. "I'm a student. It's my final year."

"He's at the university in Yokohama that I graduated from two years ago. We were in the baseball team together. I was the captain."

Shin spoke. "I teach, too, in my spare time."

"Do you?"

Sam burst out laughing. He rolled around on the bunk mak-ing a noise like a barking dog. Shin's expression darkened but he said nothing. Sam finally calmed down, wiping his eyes and whimpering.

"Tell her what you teach."

Shin rubbed his neck."I teach aerobics at the local gym."

Sam spluttered. "Imagine. Jumping up and down with all those women in leotards."

Shin's hand moved up to the side of his chin, covered a faint patch of acne.

"I've tried it." Runa smiled at Shin. "It's much harder than it looks. You'd have to be fit to teach it."

"You do have to be fit." Shin nodded appreciatively and his face disappeared behind the paper cup.

"You wouldn't catch me teaching aerobics." Sam had stretched out with his legs wide apart and his arms behind his head.

Runa watched as he stared at the wall. He was miles away but not in a daze, as she would be. His pupils were darting from side to side as if, whatever he was thinking, it was fast and absorbing. He might be having a conversation in his head.

Shin drank up his sake. Runa took the bottle and poured more for him.

"Don't give him all of it," Sam snapped and sat up to measure the amount in Shin's cup.

Runa laughed. "Sorry."

Shin took the bottle from her hand and filled up her glass then added a splash to Sam's. She wondered if she would manage to have a conversation with them that didn't involve the humiliation of Shin. She was curious to know what had sparked their fight.

"The sake is good."

"It's not my favorite kind." Sam was lying back on the bed, sipping slowly.

"I like it." Shin shuffled on the other bunk to get comfortable. Sam kicked him.

"No one asked you."

"I wasn't answering anyone. I was just saying."

Runa tried again. "I'm not sure exactly what I'm going to do in China. I've got a friend in Shanghai. I wonder if I'll be able to find her."

"You've got her address?"

"I've got it, but I don't know how to find the street. Do you know Shanghai well?"

She took Ping's address from her pocket.

"No. But I know a bit. Show me." Sam took the paper, unfolded it. "That can't be it."

"It is. What's wrong with it?"

"That's not a home address. It's the name of a hotel."

"Are you sure?"

"Definitely. That's what it says. Have you mixed it up with another piece of paper?"

"No. This is it. And it's her handwriting."

"Maybe she's staying at this hotel?"

"But she wrote this seven years ago."

"Her family run a hotel?"

"No. I'm sure they don't."

"Oh dear. You really must have got something wrong. Do you have her phone number?"

"Yes, but—"

"Well then, all you need to do is give her a call and find out where she is. Shanghai's a big city but there you go, Eriko."

"Eriko?"

"Is that not your name? What did you say your name was?"

"I don't think I did. My name is Nanao."

Runa was about to explain that she had already tried the telephone number when she noticed a figure in the doorway. It was the man who wanted to make her speak English.

She didn't pay much attention to him at first. She was trying to absorb the news that Ping had given her a false address. She did have a faint memory of Ping mentioning a hotel. Had she said something about staying in one for a few days before returning to her family. Or was Runa's mind inventing this now? But when Sam and Shin introduced themselves to the man, she took a closer look. He seemed shocked to see her there. His mouth opened wide and, because his nose was large and sharp, the effect was of a beak. Runa was reminded of some leggy bird, a heron.

"Hello, all." He entered, tentatively. "I'm in this cabin, too."

She saw how nervous he was introducing himself to his roommate. Sam's English was good. She hoped the heron would leave soon because she didn't want to keep pretending she didn't speak much English. She wished she had never decided to be Nanao. It wasn't going to help her and gave her too much to think about. She would finish her sake and leave. It didn't taste right in a toothbrush glass anyway.

"Hello there Nanao," he said, as if she were a little girl.

"Oh. Hello." She talked in a voice that was more breath than muscle. It made her sound a little more like her sister.

He sat on his bunk. Shin moved to the floor. Ralph picked something off the blanket—a magazine or catalog with English on the front—and flipped it quickly over, concealing the English. Runa had noticed the magazine but had taken no notice of its title. On the back though, were sentences in several East Asian languages. Perhaps Ralph thought that the Chinese, Thai, and Korean characters were just pretty patterns and that if he couldn't understand them, no one else would be able to.

The top one was Japanese and it said, *Oriental Brides for English Gentlemen. Interviews and Mail Order*. Runa looked away. She wanted to laugh and she wanted to hit him. Now she wondered if he had been flirting with her before. When he was promising to teach her English, was he making a move? Did she think she might marry him? Surely not. Ralph glanced at her just as she was looking at him. Their eyes caught for a second and she knew from the shine in his that she was his target. She shivered. Before, she had thought that the heron was a sweet old man but now she found him a little disturbing.

"I think I'm going for a nap. Drinking during the day, you know . . ."

She must get away from him. She needed to think about Ping, why the address was wrong. It was a problem that she had to solve before they reached Shanghai. There was no time to deal with this man, his strange book or whatever it was, and his English lessons.

"Would you like me to walk you back to your cabin?"

"No, thank you." She must remember to keep her English basic.

"It's no trouble." He was on his feet and was holding the door open for her. "Mustn't leave a lady wandering around on her own."

He followed her into the corridor and padded along just behind.

She yawned. "I've very tired."

"Were you all right in there?"

"Yes, fine." She yawned again, tried to sound bored as well as tired.

"Of course, I'm sure you were having a nice time. I was just concerned, you know, about a woman being in a room with two men she doesn't know."

Runa didn't answer.

He raised the volume and spoke slowly. "I said, I worried about you. In there. With two men."

They went down a flight of stairs and Runa found the door to her room. He was still right behind her. She wanted to turn and scream at him but she walked steadily and said nothing. Nanao would not tell him to get lost, he would just know. She hoped there would be other people in the room.

There were clothes, books, and shoes all over the tatami and shelves, but there were no people. A silky pink negligee was spread over the space next to Runa's. She felt she ought to remember the woman it belonged to, but she didn't.

She pointed to her own futon.

"I sleep here," she said and wished instantly that she hadn't. He was standing close behind her, not touching but hovering. He was thin, gangly and looked far taller than he actually was. His legs were about ten centimeters too long for his body. His arms almost reached his knees. And he looked sick. She couldn't say exactly how, but his skin was an odd color and had a clammy, congealed quality. He smelled of baby soap or shampoo.

"Very cozy. You'll have a nice sleep here. Now is very quiet."

"Yes. I hope so."

He pushed the mat with his fingertips. "Is this what they call tatami? I've never seen it before. Is it nice to sleep on?"

"Yes. It's soft."

"How lovely." He chuckles. "The traditional ways are the best, aren't they? There's really no need for big bulky beds when you think about it. But what about the other people in here? It's not mixed, is it? I wouldn't want to think there were men sleeping in here, too."

"No. Only women." She wished she could tell him otherwise, just to see his face.

She thought for a second of the man that she and Ping had beaten up, the pain on his face, the bewilderment in his piggy features as he staggered, lost on his own doorstep. How she had hated him but also how deeply she pitied him. She didn't understand it but she had the same painful mixture of feelings now for Ralph. He swayed from one foot to the other, wrinkling his nose. His pink eyes watered. What kind of woman would want him for a husband? Even using catalogs, you had to have something to offer, surely. But she knew the answer. The kind of woman whose only desire was a ticket to another country. A woman who had little going for her at home, who, perhaps, was being chased by danger. Runa sat on the edge of the tatami. This was too much. It was as if someone—Ping?—had sent the heron to her as a joke solution to her problem.

A joke, but nonetheless a possible solution.

She looked up at his tearful, irritated eyes and smiled right into them. She let him see her perfect white teeth, her soft dimples. There was a flush of excitement and confusion in his face. She broadened her smile, just a touch, until she knew she had him. This was so easy; she could do it in her sleep.

Twenty

The cabin felt different. Last night Ralph hadn't heard his cabin-mate come in, had no idea who he was. Now he knew. His name was Sam. He spoke good English, he had an odd relationship with his odd friend, and he knew Nanao. All of that made him a strong presence up there on the top bunk. Ralph was finding it hard to relax and it was far too early to sleep.

It had been upsetting to find Nanao in the cabin with those two hooligans, as if they were all friends. He wondered if she had known them before the fight—it would explain why she tried to stop them—but he thought not. She should have had more sense than to hang around with strangers who were clearly volatile. Just because they were all the same nationality didn't mean they needed to form a clique and sit around drinking together like lifelong chums.

Although he wasn't happy, he knew he had done the right thing. He'd stepped forward, reclaimed her, and taken her away.

She was sleepy. Now that he thought about it, she always seemed sleepy. But she was happy enough to walk with him. She was there, breathing gently and sweetly as they moved from one side of the boat to the other.

Then she had done something strange. A good thing, he had no doubt, but surprising. She showed him where she slept on the tatami. As she talked, she stared ahead, expressionless and vacant. She looked just like the girl in the department store elevator. He reached out to touch the place on the tatami where her body would lie. He wanted to know how it felt, wanted to connect with her sleep. And when his fingers were creeping close to the fair hairs on her calf, she looked right into his eyes and smiled. She was beautiful. Her eyes grew wider as he looked into them. Her skin glinted and he just wanted to touch her cheek, to cup her face in the palm of his hand and hold it. He sat beside her and immediately his whole head began to itch. She said the tatami was very clean, but it must have been full of dust or mites. Within seconds his eyes were streaming and he was sneezing and snorting. He groped in his pockets for a handkerchief but couldn't find one. He was sure she would be disgusted and turn away, undoing all his work. But Nanao produced a soft white handkerchief, silently held it over his nose. He wanted to take it from her but was too confused and did nothing. She gave his nose a gentle squeeze and wiped away the snot. She smiled at him. He stared back, shocked.

He couldn't remember what had happened to the hankie. He knew that he had said goodnight in a voice so low it didn't sound like his own. Her touch had left him trembling. But he felt strangely healed and warm, so he asked her to say goodnight in Japanese. She whispered it in the doorway. *Oyasumi-nasai.* Almost touching his cheek with hers.

He dreamed of taking her home and putting her in his house. He would make her a princess. He'd show her off to people in the streets and take her shopping for pretty clothes. Barry would have to eat his words. Now that he almost had her, he was a little scared. She was the girl he had been looking for all along; what if he did something wrong? He remembered her smile, her fingers tenderly on his nose. He was doing as well as he could, so he must make himself enjoy it. *Wait till you see me, Barry. Wait till you see me.*

Look, Ralph had said to his half-brother before he left England. It was early in the morning, and Barry was making toast in the kitchen. Barry had come over for the weekend so that Ralph could show him what needed doing while he was away. They'd played in the garden with the hose, examined the window locks. Then they had watched a couple of videos and had some beers. Now they were both a little hung-over.

Ralph showed his brother a photograph.

"It's my fiancée," he said. "We're getting married."

Barry turned toward him, took and scrutinized the picture. He looked as if he was searching for something polite to say.

"What's her name?"

Ralph took this as a possible sign of approval. "Li Hua. I'm meeting her in Shanghai. We're going to spend some time together. And then we'll get married, as soon as we can."

"Are you in love with her?" Barry peered through his straggly bangs, ready to disapprove.

"Very much so. Well, I suppose I don't know for certain."

"You don't know?" Barry stuck a knife into the toaster to pull the toast out.

"That's dangerous. Turn it off first. I haven't met her yet."

"Oh."

"I found her on the Internet. It wasn't just that I found the first one I could, you know. I looked at others. I'm going to meet a few in Japan, but I liked the sound of Li Hua too."

"You found her on the Internet?"

"And she's the one."

Barry's face showed nothing at all. It was a shame. Ralph had hoped to impress Barry, make him a little jealous. Maybe somewhere behind that greasy hair he was impressed. It was impossible to tell with Barry.

He pointed at Li Hua's face. "Is she pretty?"

Barry was surprised. "Why are you asking me?"

Ralph shrugged. "I don't like looking at the picture. I can see what she looks like while I'm looking at it, and then I forget what she looks like straight away. I don't want to know what she really looks like until we meet. She'll be at the port waiting for me. Love at first sight." And then he was mortified for saying, *love at first sight.*

"I see."

"So, is she pretty?"

Barry tilted his head to one side.

"Is she?"

"She looks like a man." He had already put the picture down and was looking out at the garden. "You want to get that garage door looked at before you go."

"Don't say that."

"Sorry, but it could come off in a storm."

"No. Don't say that my fiancée looks like a man."

"I'm not saying she's unattractive. It isn't that, but she looks like a man. See for yourself."

"No. That's very unkind of you."

He thought of the transvestites in Bangkok. Could Li Hua be a man? But what would be the point of a transvestite wanting to marry him? For his money, perhaps, or his British citizenship?

"It's up to you. You asked my opinion. Aren't you having any breakfast?"

"Yes. I am. I'll get something now. I'm not that bothered about the garage."

He was confused. He returned the photograph to his wallet. Of course, if Li Hua did look like a man she couldn't be a transvestite. The point about transvestites, he reminded himself, was that they looked like, very much like women, more so than many women, particularly the ones Barry tended to go out with. Barry was probably jealous that he hadn't thought of doing this. His girlfriend, Meg, was a bus driver, of all things, and expected Barry to arrange his life around hers. Barry never seemed to mind, but he must have felt a pang seeing Ralph preparing to fly off to bring back better things.

"What did happen to Apple?"

"She went back to Thailand. I told you at the time. I still haven't heard anything from her."

"Why'd she do that? What did you do?"

"Me? I brought her here, gave her a house and home, a new life. That's what I did."

"All sounds perfect. But she went off, just like that."

"She was homesick."

"You could have gone to Thailand."

"Come on. Why would I want to live there? You know what I'm like in the heat, and mosquitoes love me."

Barry rolled his eyes. "OK. But she could have gone back to visit and still lived here. Homesickness seems a very small reason to end a marriage."

"For your information, culture shock is a very serious thing. People have breakdowns, commit suicide, all kinds of things, from culture shock. But it wasn't just that." Ralph concentrated on finding plates and knives. He took them carefully from the cupboards and placed them on the table, keeping his back to Barry. "If you really want to know, Apple had an affair. We broke up over it and she left."

"Who with?"

"I don't know. I just know she had one. She told me about it."

"That doesn't sound nice. Sorry."

"Not your fault. I made her pack her bags and leave. I don't know what happened to her after that. That's why it's taken so long to get the divorce. That's why I'm going to marry Li Hua and why I'd like some support."

"You've got it."

"Good."

"But still. You don't want to rush into anything."

"I know that. I've been going very slowly with Li Hua."

"You don't know her."

"But I soon will. Don't worry. I won't make the same mistake twice."

And while Li Hua was certainly something better, there was no doubt that she was not the best possible.

Nanao. What was it about the way she said her name? It sounded strange, too emphatic, as if she expected you to disagree.

Still, he didn't know if he could trust her yet. *Steady now. Remember Apple.* She may be manipulating him, somehow. He didn't know how, but he felt her control over him like little wires being pulled. It could be love and it could be that she was another Apple. You could never tell.

He found himself standing, putting on his shoes, stepping out of the cabin. He had no idea where he was going.

Wu was passing with Mei Ling at his side. He saw Ralph and caught his sleeve.

"Hello, Ralph. Go outside. You can see dolphins."

"Pardon?"

"In the sea. Go and look. You'd better hurry."

The sea today was a soft blue sheet. Ralph scoured the water with his eyes until he thought he would pierce it. And then he saw the dolphins, close behind the ferry. Wet and rubbery they jumped and slipped between the waves. Water flicked from their tails. Ralph would have loved to touch one. He felt he could just climb over the boat's side and walk over to them. He tried to count them but they moved too fast.

His mother always said that when she watched a ballerina or

a gymnast, as long as she kept still she found herself believing that she could leap as high, turn as fast. She believed that whatever they could do, so could she. Ralph had never understood. He knew what his body would and wouldn't do. But now he watched the acrobatics on the sea and believed he could swim through the waves, twist and turn gracefully, swim forever without being tired or needing a destination. The water was so peaceful. He would sketch the scene but not yet. He would watch until the dolphins were out of sight and later see if he could capture them on paper. He thought that perhaps he could.

It wouldn't hurt to try to be a little more like his mother, from time to time. She was always looking for things that charmed her and was beautiful herself. She encouraged Ralph to draw pictures, though he never thought they were much good. She traveled all over Europe to paint and sketch, skipping off with Ralph's stepfather, and leaving Ralph at home with Barry. He hated it when they returned, full of their trip, full of their love for each other. Ralph and Barry could only watch. She was too distant from them; they couldn't touch her. She would have loved the dolphins, though.

Nanao had appeared beside him. From nowhere, like a scrap of paper blown over by the breeze, she was there. She edged forward until she was standing in front of him, not quite touching. Ralph smiled to himself. He put one arm on the boat's railing so that it was almost around her, then waited as she moved closer. There were inches between them, but somehow he could feel her, the shape of her body against his. He tried to keep his breathing steady. He needed to keep this moment in his grasp. She twisted around and looked up at him.

"Very beautiful," she said.

And he took her hand. The previous night when he saw her hand, it had been cold and stiff. Today her skin radiated golden warmth. He felt the liquid wrinkles on the insides of her knuckles, rubbed his thumb gently across her palm. His heart was drumming fast. Now that he had her hand he was not sure what to do next. Imagine if he could have made such a move with the girl in the elevator. Nanao simply stood there, allowing him to hold her. She was so demure, so quietly there. She was waiting for him to speak first, and he must. He must say something, anything.

"I think it's called a pod."

"Pardon?" She opened her eyes wide, waiting to be taught.

"A group of dolphins like this is called a pod. A pod of dolphins."

She nodded and turned back to the water, a gentle smile on her lips. "You know many things."

An hour later he was sitting on his bed, still glowing. Sam was not there. Ralph was saying her name, again and again, trying to say it the way she did. There was something so odd and mysterious in the way she said, *My name is Nanao*. He took off his glasses to rub his nose and as the cabin went into a fog he suddenly saw something clearly. She was lying. Her name was not Nanao. She was someone else. The reason it sounded strange when she gave her name was that she was pretending to be someone called Nanao. But why would she need to lie about her first name with strangers she'd never see again? It didn't make sense.

Twenty-one

*K*araoke. *Would you believe it, Nanao? Here on the boat.* Runa
talked aloud to her reflection as she brushed her hair before bed. Her eyes, usually perfect cut jet, were black and blurry,
as if painted into her face by a child. Her lips were uneven. But
how could she have stopped herself singing, drinking too
much? She wanted to have fun.

She splashed her face with water, glanced back at her eyes but
couldn't hold her reflection still. It reeled and wobbled. She
cleaned her teeth and sat on the edge of the tatami to dry her
face. Two young women were already sleeping. Both were face
down so all Runa could see was tangled black hair on the white
pillows. They were images of her sleeping self. A middle-aged
woman entered, nodded, and then began to undress and change
into flowery pyjamas. Runa scratched her leg. Something had
bitten her. There were small spots of blood on her ankle.

She crawled under the top futon, curled up in the soft cotton.
Her head was heavy and sank deep into the pillow. She shut her

eyes and felt as if she were spinning. She had no sense of the boat's rocking, only her own. She rolled onto her side. What had happened tonight? Bits of the conversations were coming back while others had disappeared. What if the pieces that wouldn't come back were the important ones? She knew that he'd asked her to marry him and somehow, in the idiotic language they were speaking, she had said yes. It was what she had wanted. She could trust no one who might have followed her from Japan. The heron, though, was safe.

She had gone to the bar hoping that she would find someone to talk to, but not the old woman. The ceiling was dotted with spotlights and the room was sparkly. It didn't seem like a room on a ferry. Small snatches of sea showed through gaps between the curtains, but as if on a flickering film projection. They weren't real. Runa stepped forward, looking for a face she recognized. There were fifteen or twenty people in pairs and groups at the small tables. All the faces were new and yet all were familiar. Runa felt she almost knew them and might have passed some on buses, in shops. She might have been to school with them, but they weren't quite familiar enough to be sure, to be able to walk up to any particular table and say hello. She had a feeling that everything was changing, and that was good, but when you were traveling, when you were surrounded by strangers, it was hard to make a decision and measure it against the backdrop of ordinary life. The backdrop wasn't there.

Shin and Sam whispered together at a corner table. Their faces were animated as if they were sharing a piece of amusing, malicious gossip. She moved toward them. They greeted her with smiles and welcomed her. She wanted to tell them her story, to hear them say that she should marry Ralph or that there was another answer, something she didn't know about. Perhaps, if she befriended Sam, he could help her find her way in China. But they were engrossed in the karaoke menu, selecting songs for themselves, and bickering about the titles. Runa was frustrated. Since first meeting them she felt she was on the edge of becoming a friend yet somehow could not come close to them. Sam glanced at her often, but Shin would keep distracting him with some comment or suggestion that seemed intended to provoke a snapped response. They were perfectly pleasant to Runa, but too wrapped up in themselves to let her in.

The two friends stepped up to the microphones, and Runa was alone at the table. She watched as Sam punched numbers into the karaoke machine with an expression of glee. Shin shuffled around behind with his arms folded. They sang a duet, a bouncy pop song that Runa had never heard before. She tapped her foot and waited for them to finish but when the song ended, they started another. Shin's voice was deep and rich. Above it Sam's was metallic and tuneless. Runa bought herself a beer and drank it steadily. She aimed to reach the bottom of the glass just as the song ended but the beer finished first. When her glass was empty she stood to go to the bar, but Sam grabbed her and put the microphone into her hand. The song was an old one that she remembered her father listening to, a man singing to his wife on their wedding day. It was an odd choice and she felt strange singing along. She couldn't see the words very clearly on the screen and wondered if her eyes needed testing. She lost her place and began to laugh. She knew she sounded terrible, but without Jun Ikeda at her side, she didn't want to sing well or to enjoy it particularly. She finished a line and let Shin take over. No one in the bar paid much attention. She forgot about her second drink and returned to her table. She didn't plan to sing again but enjoyed the colored lights on the ceiling, the warm feeling that the passengers had come alive at last and were making the boat their own.

Would she soon be married to one of them? When Nanao married Hiroshi, Runa was delighted. They were the perfect couple, both so attractively clever and gentle. She couldn't have wanted more for her sister, but Runa had been scared, too. She never admitted it but she was afraid that Nanao might not have time for her anymore, and she would be lonely. It turned out not to matter because Hiroshi was sent abroad by his company for months at a time, and when he was at home, he was friendly to Runa, always helpful and never minded the two sisters going off together. After a year or two, Runa went to the mountains to be a teacher and only saw them every few months. So she became used to Hiroshi and liked him but still, she felt the family had expanded enough and she never thought of marrying. Nanao told her to think of the future, but Runa couldn't. And here was Ralph. As long as she thought of the marriage as a bargain and nothing more, it would be all right; she could stand him. Ralph would have what he wanted, for a couple of years. And no one was ever promised a happy marriage. Even her parents—who did their very best to be happy and succeeded for many years— couldn't prevent tragedy from rotting them away. What she was about to do was no different from compensated dating, just an arrangement, just longer term.

When Sam and Shin were singing, she noticed that the wound on Sam's temple had opened slightly and was glistening as though it had only just stopped bleeding. She tried to avert her eyes—it was rude to stare—but he was singing with such enthusiasm that she couldn't look anywhere but at him. Blood began to drip down his cheek. She focused instead on his mouth, as if the rest of his face wasn't there, watched it open, shut, make shapes around words, but soon the red snake slipped onto his lips, changed shape, and spread over them. The song ended and he smiled widely. The blood smeared across his face. Runa was trembling. She applauded, hoping he would go and attend to the wound, but he stood still. Shin helped him to Runa's table. He was expecting her to do something about the blood, but she had given her handkerchief to the heron so there wasn't much she could do. Why was she mopping up everyone's fluids today?

"Sorry. I'm not much good at looking after people. I'm not quite sure what to do."

"It's his own fault. He tried to start another fight before we came in here. You know, he's not very strong. I didn't bother to hit him back this time but by then his face was already hurt."

Shin took Sam's hair tenderly, held it back from the blood. Sam attempted feebly to move Shin's hand, but gave up and let his arm droop.

"I do hope it heals up soon."

"He'll be all right." Shin was propping Sam up against the back of the seat.

"Shut the fuck up and get me a towel or some water." Sam

spat blood and saliva as he spoke. "Otherwise I won't be all right, will I? I'm bleeding here, if you hadn't noticed."

"Come on then, stupid. Let's get you sorted out."

"Don't call me stupid. Who the hell are you?" His eyes screwed up in pain and more red tears trickled down his cheek. His voice rasped. "You're just an aerobics instructor. You're the brainless one. I'm the high school teacher."

"Are you?" Runa was shocked.

"Yes, for your information, I am. I teach sports and I know a thing or two about injuries so I really would appreciate some water. Now."

Shin led him away to the bathroom. Runa moved to a different table, one without splashes of blood. She turned her back on the karaoke for a while and looked out at the sea. The sight tired her. After a while you started to forget what land was, what it was like to pass a stranger on the street, to cycle through trees in the shadows of mountains, to set off on a path and walk for miles. When she returned to Japan—whenever that would be— she would go by plane. She felt a pang of homesickness, afraid that now she had left, somehow she wouldn't be able to get back again. Like the school—now that she couldn't see her country, it didn't exist. But where did that leave her sister? *Nanao, watch out for me. Don't disappear.*

Shin and Sam had gone and Runa was alone. Sam was a high-school teacher. Now she could never tell him her story. She knew what he would think of her. She might as well say, *Hey, I'm a criminal, I'm a weirdo.* She imagined Sam in the school she had come from, leading the boys across the sports field, blowing his whistle, running tired through rain and snow.

Her mind moved to the sports teachers she remembered—
including Kawasaki—in the staffroom, strutting around in their
tracksuits, now accusing her of every evil, speculating on her
escape.

A woman was singing a Chinese song. Her voice was high
and sharp. Runa was reminded of a seagull. The music swelled
around the sound and for a moment the boat and its noise
seemed to expand together. Runa thought about Sam and was
scared. He would judge her, but it was worse than that. Sam was
a high-school teacher, a former university baseball captain, just
like Kawasaki. He even went to university in Yokohama, as
Kawasaki had. He would be the coach of the school baseball
team. Was it possible that Sam and Kawasaki knew each other,
that Kawasaki had taken the photograph and then sent Sam to
follow her? Perhaps, when they whispered together, when they
fought, it had something to do with Runa.

Ralph appeared. He had a drink in each hand.

"I've got you a glass of wine. Nice singing back there." His
own drink was beer.

"Thank you."

He must have been watching her from a corner or from outside the room. She shuddered. He had been jealous before, when
he found her in his cabin with Sam and Shin, but Runa was a
step ahead of the heron.

He placed the glasses on mats, a little too carefully, as if he
were used to a lifetime of compensating for natural clumsiness.
He sat beside her. She could see that he was trying to think of
something to say. She felt sorry for him.

"I live in a town called Carlisle."

"I don't know Carlisle."

"It is a small, friendly town. It is near the Lake District. Very beautiful lakes and high mountains. I like climbing them." He mimed climbing a mountain and she smiled at him. He grinned back. He looked so confident, suddenly, as if he wasn't used to being smiled at for what he said. "Though not very high ones."

"Near your house?" she asked, wondering if she could now admit that she spoke pretty good English. She had a feeling that he preferred her without it, liked the game of baby talk. He was the kind of man who would take you out for dinner and try to cut up your food and feed it to you with your own fork, but do nothing to lift a finger in his own house. It would be better not to mention that she was a qualified teacher.

"Yes. Very near my house. Beautiful mountains and lakes. Do you like the countryside?"

"Yes. I like."

"My house isn't quite in the countryside but it has a big garden. And a garden shed. My house has a lot of rooms. It is warm, too."

"Warm?"

"Yes. The heating system is new. In winter it gets dark early. I like to close all the windows and turn the heating very high." He was miming each action to make himself clear. "I draw pictures and read books, mostly picture books. Or I listen to music in the dark."

"It's nice."

"But I get lonely in the dark. I like to share things. People need to share."

"I think so."

"My house is very big for just one person, Nanao."

"It is?"

"I'm not married. I'm single, you see. How about you?"

"Yes. Me, too." He had asked her the same question before. He must be very nervous.

"I was married before. My wife was from Thailand."

"You are married now?"

"No. She went away. She wasn't a good person but I'd like to marry again."

"Me, too."

He clasped her hand. She looked at their fingers, all scrunched together, and felt tears welling. But she didn't know what they were for, and she excused herself to go to the toilet. She stood and had to steady herself by clutching the tables as she walked. Instead of rocking, the boat seemed to be pulsating, the people getting bigger and smaller, the colors growing bright and then dimming, with each beat. Outside the bar, she found the door with a little triangular woman on the window. She was about to push it when Sam's head appeared in front of hers. Half of his face was covered by a paper towel, glued to his skin with a blot of ruby red. Why were they so violent? She was certain that he must be a friend of Kawasaki's. She recognized the gratuitous bullying of the playing field. Kawasaki had asked them to follow her as some kind of favor.

"Are you all right?" she asked him.

"Are you all right?" he parroted, looking at Runa strangely as if noticing her for the first time.

"No, I'm asking you. Your injury looked bad."

"No, I'm asking you."

"What?"

"I'm asking you. You're talking to that British guy again. It seems to be getting serious. I think he's after you. You want to watch out."

"It's fine. I like him."

"Really? You like him?" Sam stared in disbelief.

"Yes. What's wrong with that?"

"Nothing." He shrugged. "Nothing at all. He seems a bit old for you. I thought a pretty woman like you would prefer someone younger."

"I don't see what you mean."

His black eyes flickered, darted around her face. "But wouldn't you? Wouldn't you prefer a younger man?"

Shin came and pulled him away. Runa went through the door and almost fell into a cubicle. She put down the lid of the toilet and sat to think. The walls and floor were turning now, like pieces in a kaleidoscope. Yes, she would prefer a younger man and Sam seemed to know it. There was no need for either of them to say Jun's name now. Sam was watching her.

She returned to the bar and looked around for Ralph. A young Chinese woman had taken over at the microphone and was singing Madonna songs. Runa stared for a few minutes, admiring her voice, the slinky way she moved while she sang, without quite dancing. She watched, in fact, until a bony body obstructed her view.

The heron was back, now with a whole bottle of wine, and before Runa could twist her head to see him clearly, her glass was full to the brim. He put his face close to hers and his lips spread into a grin. Pinheads of sweat glistened in his pores. Runa looked down and swallowed. Then she reached out her hand and moved a strand of sticky hair from his forehead, pushed it back. She felt herself blush. And then somehow they were talking about marriage. *When we go to England,* he was saying. And a few minutes later, *as soon as we're married.* So all she had to do was spend some time with him, get to England, and live with him. It would be hard, probably impossible, to marry him with just Nanao's passport for identification, but at least she would get there and have somewhere to live for a while. He was saying that she could start on a tourist visa and then, if necessary, he would get her a student visa, just until they could sort out the marriage. He would pay for her to do a course. Cooking or flower arranging. Ralph had planned every detail and he didn't seem to require an answer. She only had to nod and smile. Still, she was a little scared by the size of the lie.

Ralph had brought other people to their table. Shin and Sam, Wu and Mei Ling, and there were other faces behind theirs. He clinked his glass against the bottle.

"Ladies and gentlemen, I have an announcement to make." He was stooping to the left and swaying slightly. A section of his hair stuck out, like a wing, from the side of his head. He spoke slowly, concentrating hard on enunciating his words correctly.

"Nanao and I have just decided to become engaged. We're having a little romantic drink to celebrate and I invite you all to join us."

He started pulling chairs around the table, beckoning everyone in the bar to sit down and hold out their glasses. Runa had no idea whether or not they understood his English, but most looked baffled. Sam stared at Runa. She tried not to notice and focused instead on Ralph, smiling sweetly to show Sam—and Ralph—how happy she was. Around her were faces, all packed together like pieces of sushi in a box. She could no longer make out their expressions.

"I see this boat," Ralph swished his glass from left to right, "as a symbol of our new life together, our journey into the unknown waters of our love." Then he whispered to Runa, "I'm going to write a haiku for you, Nanao, to show you my feelings in poetry."

Again she smiled.

Ralph began to talk to Wu and Mei Ling. The alcohol was making him louder and more energetic, whereas Runa was becoming quieter and more tired.

"Nanao, darling." He turned to her. "Are you happy?"

"Yes. Happy." She smiled and held it.

"Don't ever lose your beautiful smile." He ran a leathery finger over her lips. "It's such a beautiful smile."

She kept smiling. She couldn't think of anything else to do.

"And when we get to England, we will plan so many things together. Me and you, apple. We'll be a happy couple together in our nest."

When they reached Shanghai, when she was away from the prying eyes of the other passengers, she could always try one last time to contact Ping, somehow.

Sam and Shin were deep in conversation, again. She watched them. Sam glanced at her a couple of times and she knew that they were discussing her. If only she and the heron could get off the boat now and disappear. But Shin, Sam, the old woman, they'd be with her all the way to Shanghai. All she had to do was stop the old woman or Sam talking to the heron and telling him who she was. One way would be to stay with the heron all night and make sure he spoke to no one. But he shared a cabin with Sam. She could lure the heron from the cabin to sleep with her, but he would think she wanted sex. Alternatively, she could do something about Sam.

Now it seemed that the ferry was speeding up, bumping up on the waves, sinking forward then up again. Runa wanted to ask the captain to make it go even faster. She could hear Kawasaki's voice, *I would wring her neck*, and she knew that he had meant it. Now that she was far from home, she knew that Kawasaki was the letter writer because there was no other suspect. He had seen her with Jun and was jealous. She remembered returning to her apartment early one morning, kissing Jun goodbye behind the gym, and two minutes later walking into Kawasaki who was preparing for practice. Only now did she understand the expression on his face, pure hate disguised as indifference. He had seen, of course he had, but she had been too carefree to notice. But what now? Sam could stop her going with the heron, or he could let her go and report back to Kawasaki, which seemed pointless. Would he hurt her? She couldn't believe that Sam was capable of real harm. She thought that his irritability was an act. Yet, all that fighting, the blood. Sam and Shin were, as Nanao would say with her head to one side, *a little . . . just a little . . .*

Runa got up. The older woman was now sleeping. Runa looked at her face. Was she the woman from the bath? She looked younger but, from above, it was difficult to tell. Runa hadn't noticed her here last night. Or perhaps she had and that was why the woman had seemed familiar in the bath, and she had nothing to do with the school. Runa saw that a couple of other passengers had entered and gone to bed around her while she was thinking.

If Jun Ikeda were the person she had to marry in order to find an escape, would it be easier? Would it be easy? No, it would be hard. He was an ordinary schoolboy in a dull navy uniform. He fitted the bill for a while, but now he didn't seem special, just terribly young. And that was funny because Jun was the root of the trouble, the beginning of the escape.

She put her hand into her bag. The knife was there. She grasped the cloth and let her fingers close around it. She wouldn't know how to stab a person even in self-defense. The thought of pushing a blade through a person's skin and into their flesh made her nerves scream. If Sam or Shin attacked, though, she would have to look after herself. She could cut their arms. She would only hurt them seriously if she had to. If they didn't stop, she'd push the knife in.

She unwrapped it, just enough to feel the blade inside the bag. It was only a small penknife and she didn't know how sharp it was. But what *would* it feel like to stab a person? The touch of cold metal snapped her from her reverie like smelling salts. This was madness. She was tingling all over. She must find Sam.

Twenty-two

R alph was in heaven. The bar, with its booming karaoke and garish lights, was strangely cozy. All those people celebrating together. Strangers were better than friends. You would think that at such a moment of beauty and triumph, it would be best to be surrounded by people who knew you, but it wasn't. Ralph had discovered that the eyes of strangers, when kind and admiring, were the best of all. You could relax into the gaze, find yourself being all the things you wanted to be. And now he was engaged to Nanao. The journey back home would be his lap of honor.

The door to the deck was locked. Ralph walked to the other end and tried another. It was open. He pushed it slightly but was scared to walk through. He guessed they'd locked the other door for the night, for safety, and forgotten this one. The thought that it might be dangerous made him nervous. Was it safe to go out or not? And then he remembered what he'd pushed to the back of his mind all evening. Nanao's name. He would prefer to laugh at himself now for thinking there was anything strange about it, but he must check. It was the last item on his list of things to do. He found her, wandering near the door to his room.

"Nanao. Were you looking for me?"

"Oh, no. I was just walking." She had been checking the numbers on the doors. She must have been searching for him.

"Shall we walk together?"

"I'm not really going anywhere. I'll probably sleep very soon."

"I must say, your English is getting much better. Our conversations have had quite an effect."

"Yes." She stopped, uncomfortable. Did she look a little guilty?

"Nanao. We'll be in Shanghai soon. I thought that since we'll be going to England as soon as we've got you a ticket, Shanghai could be our honeymoon. You can go and say hello to your friend, and then we'll spend the rest of the time together. I've already arranged a hotel room and everything."

"All right."

"So we'll be doing everything backwards."

"Backwards?"

He reached forward and stroked her hair.

"And since we're doing things this way, I thought we could . . ." he stopped and put his mouth near her ear, breathing softly through his nose. "I though we might consummate our relationship now."

His fingers moved down her neck, stroking her hair and her skin. She folded her arms across her chest and stepped back.

"It's all right. Don't be afraid."

"No. I don't want to."

"There's no need to be nervous." But he was awkward now, and had no idea how to make her do what he wanted without forcing her. "Come on. We can go to the table-tennis room. It'll be empty now."

If he inhaled through his mouth he sounded as if he were hyperventilating, so he continued to breathe in and out through his nose. To his own ears, the noise was deafening. He tried to breathe silently but it came out louder and then he thought he would stop breathing altogether. Nanao was silent. Her chest rose and fell evenly, but she made no sound.

"No. I'd like to go to bed." She squeezed his hand. "I'm tired."

"There's no need for us to wait."

She rubbed the tips of his hair between her fingers, but he couldn't tell whether the gesture was real or affected. She turned to move away.

"Nanao. We don't have to wait."

"I think we should, until we're married. It's just the way I've always wanted to do it."

"Your English really is good now, isn't it, considering you could hardly speak a word before. Who are you?"

"What?" She was guilty. He could see that in the dark place behind her eyes she was trying to work out how he knew and what she could do to get out of it.

"What's your name?" His face was close to hers and a pinprick of his saliva landed on her lip when he spoke. She stepped back, looking repulsed. For a second he hated her, but he knew he mustn't be angry yet. He might still want her and couldn't afford to spoil things so soon.

"My name is Nanao. I want to go to bed. Let's talk tomorrow."

"No. You can't just change like this." His face and neck were burning. He could see the redness out of the corners of his eyes and in contrast Nanao seemed to grow colder and whiter.

"I thought you were—"

"Who? Who did you think I was?" Her eyes that he had found so beautiful before were nothing more than hard little marbles.

"I don't know. I thought you were the person I thought you were." He swallowed and blinked back tears. "But you're not. Why are you doing this to me?"

"Sleep well," she said. "There's nothing to worry about."

"I'm not going to sleep. I'm going outside."

She leaned forward to give him a peck on the cheek, but at the same time he went to the same side. Somehow his glasses slipped sideways so that one arm was way above his ear and the other was touching his chin. The room turned over with them. He fumbled quickly to put them into place. Nanao was already far down the corridor. She was rocking from side to side as she walked. He heard a sound from her, a big sigh of relief and a giggle. She was laughing at him. He slumped to the floor.

Sam sat on Ralph's bunk and congratulated him. His face was a bloodied mess.

"I hope you will be happy together."

Ralph resented Sam even speaking about Nanao and was determined not to appear grateful.

"Oh yes. I'm sure we will. I'm not worried about it. Are you married yourself?" He spoke with disdain.

"No."

"Have you not met the right woman, then?"

"My ideal woman," Sam said, moving closer to Ralph, "is the one you're going to marry. Never mind." He patted Ralph's hand. "She told me she likes you so that's all right. I don't mind."

Ralph had no idea what to say. He wasn't going to apologize or wish Sam well. He didn't need to know that Sam liked Nanao, though he had suspected that one of the pair was interested in her. He hated having his hand patted.

"She told you she liked me? You were talking about me?"

"Yes. Oh, but don't worry. I like men, too, and I have my ideal man already. I wouldn't want to be greedy. Anyway, Shin doesn't like it when I look at girls."

"What?"

"He's very jealous and loses his temper every now and again. Most of the time I keep him in his place, though. I think he's pleased that Nanao's out of my way. So, congratulations."

Ralph left the cabin. There were no safe places anymore.

Later he went to Nanao's room to find her, but her space was empty. On all the other futons, women slept. In the darkness he saw wisps of hair, pyjama sleeves, soft skin covering bony elbows, curved mounds under white covers. Silent in the doorway, he could almost smell their sleep. But where was she?

He leaned through the door, knelt down, reached for her bag. He was looking for something, anything with her name on. Perhaps a letter or an address book. It would have to be written in the Roman alphabet, not in Japanese. A wedding ring, buried at the bottom, would be a clue. He crawled backward into the corridor. He stood and groped in the bag. There was little inside, apart from some sweets and cash, but he slipped his fingers into a small zipped compartment and pulled out her passport. There was a picture of a chrysanthemum on the front. That was the Japanese national flower, so at least she was telling the truth about her nationality. He flicked through to find her name, but it said Nanao. Nanao Wada. Perhaps he had done her an injustice. Perhaps she wasn't lying. He had always been too sensitive, found it hard to trust people, because he had been let down so often. He'd done it again. He couldn't resist a glance at her photo, so he held the picture up to the light for a better view. He was looking at the face of a different woman.

He was too tired to understand this and wanted to be sober, so that he would know what to do. He leaned into the room and threw down the bag. Something glinted from the folds of her bed covers. He put out one hand and recoiled as his skin ripped open. His jaws snapped shut with pain, and he kept his teeth clenched so that he wouldn't shout out. The sleepers were beginning to stir as he backed out of the room and ran away. The bitch had a knife. He stumbled down the corridor sucking the skin between his index finger and his thumb. What the hell was she doing with a penknife lying open on her bed?

Twenty-three

T he ferry had become a swollen, tender object. She thought
that if you touched it from the outside, it would scream.

There were few people around. The bar seemed to be closing
and the last few drinkers were heading for their cabins. Once
she had shaken off the heron, Runa kept walking, turned corners in the corridors. She didn't want to see him again tonight.
First she had to confront Sam, find out who he was and what
he knew. She returned to that part of the ferry, looked at all the
cabin doors but couldn't remember which belonged to Sam and
the heron. And she'd forgotten to bring her knife. She laughed
at herself for having screwed up her own plan. She listened at
three or four doors to faint snoring, gentle creaking. You
couldn't hurt any of them, not while they were asleep.

She would go to the bathroom where she had talked to the
old woman about Ping. The bath would have been emptied for
the night or would, at least, be cold, but it was where she

wanted to be. If she imagined a room filled with scorching steam, perhaps that was what she would find.

The bathroom was open and hot water filled the tub. Runa entered the changing room and slipped off her T-shirt and leggings. It would be easier to sleep after a hot bath, easier to wake in the morning with a decision freshly made.

She sat on the wet tiles at the side of the bath, dangled her feet in the scalding water. Then she lowered her whole body, slowly, into the heat.

In England she would make new friends, perhaps meet a real husband, get a job. And after a couple of years, with new qualifications and experience, she'd return home and start afresh, get it right this time. She wouldn't be a teacher again. She'd try something new, be a journalist, or a florist. Then again, she had always thought it would be fun to have a little bookshop selling English books. Or she would open her own bar. She could reopen the Octopus, start up the karaoke machines. She would look after her guests, ensure no one was ever lonely. Or it might be better to set up an identical place in a different part of Japan. But if all those aims were impossible when she first got home, she'd take anything just to save a bit of money. She'd work in a garage, waving cars onto the forecourt. She'd work in a department store, spraying perfume on customers or pressing buttons in the elevator. She'd live near Nanao and rent a little flat in the countryside not far from the station. She'd cycle around the village doing her shopping, humming as she went. She'd fall in love for the first time in her life and it would be with someone who wouldn't desert her in the night. In the meantime she must make the most of going to England with the heron. She was not being quite honest with him, but that was OK. Runa understood what he wanted her to be, and she could be that, easily.

She was dreaming about the footbridge by the shopping center and the women who worked in the department store. She was running around the shops with Ping, being chased by shop assistants in pink uniforms. She sank further into the water and in the dream she was swimming with water bubbling around her mouth.

Runa opened her eyes and sat up straight. Her heart was beating fast, her nose was full of water. If she was not careful she would drown herself and that would be the end of her plans. She didn't know how long she'd been asleep, seconds or minutes. Her body was burning now but she felt too heavy to pull herself out.

What if she didn't marry the heron? What if she got a boat straight back to Kobe, started again in another part of Japan? But they would be looking for her, the journalists, Jun Ikeda's parents, the school authorities. Now she had used a stolen passport it was even worse; she was a genuine criminal. Her knees bent and she slipped further down, let the water lap around her chin, imagined she was in the sea, rocking along in the saltiness, just Runa and the sea and sky. She shut her eyes.

There was a noise from the direction of the corridor. Perhaps someone was coming to empty the bath for the night. It occurred to her that she hadn't checked that this was the women's bathroom and not the men's. She must have, but she didn't remember looking at the door. She hoped no one planned to join her now. These moments were hers and she wouldn't share them. The door opened but she could see nothing through the steam. She kept still and willed the intruder to leave.

A man cleared his throat. It was a weak noise, a nervous clearing or an attempt to say *I am here*, rather than a necessary shifting of phlegm. Runa looked around. There was no way out of the room except in the direction of the person. She heard him breathing, a wheezing, tired kind of breathing. Was it Ralph? She should lift herself from the water to see, but she had no towel and her clothes were out of reach. She squinted hard at the steam but could make out no shapes. Ralph always breathed heavily, but it didn't sound like him. The sound was distorted by the tiles and steam so it was hard to tell. Whoever it was, surely he would go away now that he knew there was a woman in the bath.

This may be the man she was going to marry. And she would do it but would have no more to do with him tonight. Could she pretend to be asleep in a bath? She managed to lift herself to a squatting position without making a sound but still saw no one. She spoke in Japanese.

"Actually, this is the women's bathroom. Or have I made a mistake?"

Perhaps it was the old woman again—not a man's voice at all—loving the bathtub even more than Runa did. Runa didn't want to see her again but felt safer thinking it was the woman so she waded through the water, climbed out of the other side, skidded slightly on the tiles, and stopped to steady herself. She lunged toward the changing room for her clothes. They had gone. She stood among the damp wooden shelves, protected only by a thin film of water. Now what was happening to her?

Twenty-four

She reached into the water to pull out her clothes. She was making no attempt to cover any part of her body. Ralph blinked and his whole vision turned scarlet. He put his hands on her shoulders and pushed her into the bath with her sinking clothes. There was no scream, just a cutting intake of breath that made him shudder and step back.

She cowered in the corner, squatting in the water. She was coughing and hiccuping. But he loved her. Her body was perfect, a revelation in its smooth neatness, and she had promised it to him. She was weak now and would answer him.

"Who are you?"

But she didn't answer, and then she couldn't because his hands were on her neck. He couldn't help it. Not tightly, he wasn't hurting her, just making a point. He put one hand over her mouth and picked her up, put her back in the bath. Her arms and legs were flailing all over the place and she was trying to bite his hand. He would have a couple of nasty bruises in the morning, but fortunately he had brought some lotion.

"I'm not going to force you, but you're hurting me and I want you to know what that feels like."

She coughed up water. Her face was red and her eyes were narrow, quite ugly. She spat out her words. "I don't care."

"You've made a fool out of me."

She made a strange spluttering sound, and he was afraid that he had really hurt her. But he looked at her face and saw that she was not choking, she was laughing.

"What's funny?"

"I saw that thing in your cabin. Asian brides by mail order or whatever it was. I guess I'm the perfect girl you were looking for."

She was laughing, coughing, and sobbing all at the same time.

He pulled back her hair, pushed her head down under the water, and held her there, just to make her see. All that hair turning the water's surface black, like paint dispersing. And he let the weight of his body push her down quickly, because she was small, and because she was laughing at him.

Twenty-five

Runa woke up. Jun was massaging her temples. He rubbed her skin from her shoulders down to her fingers to warm her. Then from her waist, down her legs to her toes. Stars were exploding in her head.

Jun, where am I? What's happening to me?

Nothing, he said. Let's go home. We'll go to the Octopus. Are you laughing or crying, he asked. Laughing, of course, she told him.

Something slapped against her face and neck, felt like a mosquito swatter. She pulled herself up onto her elbows and was sitting at a low table on a heated carpet. Nanao was at the other side of the table. She was excited to see Runa but kept forgetting what she was saying and didn't listen to Runa. Nanao skipped from subject to subject not covering anything, not finishing a single thing she said.

So you're getting married then, Runa, she said. We're pleased to hear it.

No, you're wrong. I've changed my mind you see. You're wrong.

And then Runa was slipping down through water, reaching up to be pulled out, but she couldn't find any other hands to grasp. She must fight to stay awake. Nanao would soon be here to help because Runa was thinking of her. She was sure that if she concentrated hard enough, Nanao would know and would come to her. *You're my sister and I will help you.*

Pictures jumped and flickered in her mind with the stars crashing around the edges. The blue-fronted café near Nanao's university. A plastic tablecloth with hard spots where it had been burned and melted. A cold glass of liquid with bubbles rising to the surface. Runa trying to open her mouth but finding nothing to say and waiting for her sister to speak. Nanao sipping a bright orange liquid, smiling. *I'm pregnant, Runa. There's going to be a baby and you're going to be an aunt. Imagine.*

You're right. That is good news.

Pain seared through her body. More pictures. A dark room with a low ceiling and no corners. Yellowed newspapers on the round table. Her father sitting with a grey blanket over his knees, his eyes on the tiny goldfish in the tank beside his chair. Calling out in a cracked voice for Runa to come and visit.

*   *   *

Her mother walking by the lake at the summer festival with fireworks, fire-flowers burning the sky. Runa and Nanao dressed in blue *yukatas*, running behind, tilting their heads back, and trying to keep their eyes on the sky. Fireflies in the night. Their mother smiling.

Runa tried to cough. They weren't stars that she saw before but exploding gunpowder, fireworks. Was her mother here with her?

Nanao in the hall telling her to go off to school. A priest bowing his head in the doorway, the curtains closed, her mother's cold body in the living room, and Ping waiting around the corner of the house to walk with Runa to the footbridge. Ping sucking in her cheeks to light a cigarette. Cars and trucks speeding past in both directions and drowning all other sound.

A little girl putting a water lily into a jar and filling it from a cold tap to give to her English teacher.

Water. The strange ferry and the tall ugly man, trying to stop her finding her friend, herself plunging a knife into his chest, pulling her body free from his. His face bulging and sweating, his spit spraying all over her face. Nanao's voice murmuring in her ears about something important. An empty wooden shelf and Runa's clothes out of reach, underwater.

*   *   *

Runa coughed and took in air. She could almost open her eyes. She was fighting to open them. *I'm crying, Nanao. Can you hear me? Make me stop. You can't imagine the pain I'm in.*

She couldn't breathe. Had she brought Nanao's knife? It must be here, somewhere near her hand. Her fingers opened and then closed around water, again and again, grasping desperately for something solid.

Twenty-six

It was clear what had happened. She'd fallen asleep and drowned. Or slipped on the tiles, fallen in, and then drowned. He could leave her in the bath where she'd died.

Apple was begging him to get out and save himself as he had before. He couldn't go out and he couldn't stay in the bathroom. He hovered over the body, looking away then looking at her. She was still beautiful and she was still a liar.

He stepped out of the misty room into the bright corridor, closed the door and stopped. It all looked the same. Everything had changed but you couldn't see it. They would find her in the morning but there might be scratches on her skin, could be bruises. His safety depended on whether or not anyone saw him enter the bathroom. Sam and his friend had been sitting on the stairs as he passed, but they were arguing, again, and would never have noticed him.

Ralph went back into the bathroom and waited an hour or two. He sat beside the bath. It was strange to be so close to an empty person. If he could just fill her up again, pump her back to life. He rocked on the floor with his knees up by his ears and didn't look at the bath. Perhaps she had been clever and escaped. He hadn't pushed her so hard, after all. When he went out of the room before, she could have crept out and hidden in the changing room, then slipped away when he returned. He couldn't have hurt her. He stood, looked at the bath as if waking up and realizing, gradually, that the horrors of the imagination in sleep weren't real. But she was there. Her face floated on the bath water's surface like a water lily in a pond. There was an intensity in her expression but of no particular kind or color. His arms and legs moved forward mechanically. He closed her eyes to let her sleep.

Enough time passed. He carried her out of the bathroom, onto the deck. The door banged open in the wind and he had to force it shut with his foot. She was heavy but he was strong. The problem was stopping her hands hurting as they dragged on the ground. The air was so cold he was almost burning. It felt good, as if he were being scoured clean. He could hear nothing. The noise of the sea was there but it was something that vibrated in his limbs, in the back of his head, not like a sound.

Ralph rested Nanao—no, she had no name—on the ferry's edge for a moment. He didn't look around to see if he was being watched; there was nothing he could do now. He was sorry that she would be so cold and wished he had dressed her again, just to give her a little warmth. He cupped his hands and blew into them to give himself courage. Then with one movement, he pushed her over. There was no splash though the drop was far, no opening up of the water to swallow her. She'd gone. The sea hadn't changed and there was nothing left of her on the boat. Ralph was alone, as before. Perhaps he was meant to be alone forever.

He turned back, walked toward his cabin, met no one. He was safe. The girl was a nobody with a stolen passport. Who would know she was missing? If someone did, how would they report it? Which name would they give? The lights in the corridor were weak now. He walked, bumping slightly from side to side as the boat tilted. It would be strange to walk on dry land again. Sam was sleeping, snoring loudly. His bruised arm hung over the edge of the bunk. Ralph changed quietly into his pyjamas and slipped under the blanket. Sam didn't stir.

When daylight came, he would be on the Huangpu River, heading into Shanghai. He would watch the city as it stretched into his view and he would plan his days of wandering, sketching, shopping, and eating. He'd look for dolphins. He might have another game of table tennis. He'd avoid Sam and Shin; they could be looking for the girl. But, he reminded himself, they were so absorbed with themselves that they would have forgotten her by then.

At some point, when the girl's room was empty of passengers, he would take her bag and dispose of it. And if he forgot, who would care? Wouldn't it just be found much later, dumped in some lost property place? It wasn't as if she had really existed in the first place. He might just keep one small thing, a souvenir, an item of clothing or the packet of sweets. He would put it with Apple's clothes and the pretty lights in the attic, to help him through long nights.

He had learned so much on this trip, had gained confidence in many things he'd found difficult before. He mustn't get upset about events he couldn't change but would focus on the good points. Tomorrow there would be no silliness or missing her. He needed to stay calm now, no outbursts or confusion.

He snuggled down into his sheets, put one hand down the front of his pyjamas, grasped the warm skin for comfort. *I've made a mistake and I'm sorry, but I still don't want to be alone forever.*

And he remembered that he had another chance. He didn't have to be alone. When he arrived in Shanghai, Li Hua would be waiting at the dock to greet him. She was going to be his wife. He'd be more careful this time, take his pills and not do anything rash. There would be nothing to worry about. He'd clutch her in his arms, there at the water's edge, and propose.

The Asian woman will bathe you, sing to you. She will always be there for you. She asks for nothing more. When you have been in love with an Eastern Blossom, you will know what we mean and we promise that you will never again settle for less.

Ralph watched the silhouette of Sam's hand as it swayed in the dark. You could become fond of something so familiar, even if you didn't like the person. Things so comfortable and cozy took the place of home when you were lost or far away. He lifted his head and looked more closely because the arm seemed too long and one finger was pointing quite definitely at the floor. It seemed a funny thing to do in sleep. He didn't want to wake Sam by touching him, but as he watched the hand he saw that it was moving and Sam was not asleep at all.

Hello Ralph. You've been out a long time this evening. What have you been up to?

Nothing much. Just out and about, you know.

With Nanao? Your friend and mine.

No, not with Nanao. She's in bed.

Is she? I looked for her there but didn't find her.

She must have been somewhere else.

You're right. She must have been in another place, after all. I'll look for her in the morning.

Good night, then.

Sleep well, Ralph. I hope you warm up soon.

Sorry?

I noticed you went outside. It must have been cold at such an hour. You wouldn't want to get sick. I hope you warm up quickly. Well, good night.

The top bunk creaked as Sam rolled over and then the arm appeared, again with a finger pointing sharply downward. Ralph stared until the finger began to turn into an object. He reached slowly, trying to make no noise, and put one finger on the edge of the object but he knew what it was before the blade flicked and sliced into his finger.

Twenty-seven

The sky has stopped banging and Nanao's voice has gone. Ping is there; pulling Runa's hands through the water and leading her to safety. The ferry has reached China. They are in Shanghai and Runa follows Ping through the dark streets. Crowds move around them noisily, blurred at the edges like ink blots. Ping lights a cigarette and holds it out but Runa's fingers can't feel anything so it falls to the ground and goes out. They are at the doors of a shopping center, dizzyingly bright and warm. Runa wants to step through the doorway after Ping and toward the beautiful shops, but feels that she has misplaced something and won't be able to enter until she has found it. She remembers the water lily at school and the smiling girl who held it out to her, but the flower falls to pieces and the petals float away. Her fingers move through the air and water but there is nothing to grasp.

The season has turned and it is cold. She can feel neither water nor air. Her neck is loose but sleep is near. Her bed rocks harder and she sinks into its softness, reminded of home.